BAD MOVIE NIGHT

PATRICK LACEY

Grindhouse Press
PO BOX 540
Yellow Springs, Ohio 45387

Grindhouse Press #095
ISBN-13: 978-1-957504-08-7

For Nora, who keeps the static away.

ONE

IT'S FRIDAY AND YOU KNOW what that means.

You and Ray and the rest of the gang will order takeout, split a six-pack (or drink one each), and sit in front of the television in the screening room. The couch is falling apart, hardly screen-ready anymore, but you've held off on tossing it. It's a leftover from your college days. You found it on the side of the road and even then it looked old. The springs poke through the fabric like sprouting teeth and the cotton filling sticks to everything. But it's molded to you and throwing it away feels dirty.

You're good at holding on, especially when you should let go.

You've been in the editing suite all afternoon, working on the next video. Each one grows more complicated, with clips from the films scattered throughout. And the jokes fall flat if you don't cut a frame too early. They say comedy is all about timing and they're right, because none of you is particularly funny. You've lost track of the day. It's nearly six and the boys will be by soon. But you've got a deadline. The fans are always hungry for more content and you don't want to disappoint. They're the ones who keep the lights on. And besides, you *like* editing, like the way you can manipulate a video to make others feel what you want them to. You wish you could do that with reality.

If all goes well, you'll be ready to upload by tomorrow. One video a week. That's what you promised the fans after you hit one million subscribers on YouTube. A milestone even if you'd do this for free in a friend's basement. That's how it started anyway, the channel and the reviews of bad movies. YouTube gave you a silver plaque to commemorate the occasion. It's around here somewhere, among the thousands of VHS tapes and bootleg DVDs. You think you saw it downstairs last week, where you store the sets, but things have a way of moving around on their own in this place.

You break for a cup of coffee even if it's a lost cause. Two hours from now you'll be well on your way to getting obliterated. While it's brewing, you tap your foot and whistle and do anything to break the silence because true silence isn't something you've known for a long time. For you, silence is agony. Silence is the constant ringing in your ears, the tinnitus that's supposed to get worse with caffeine and alcohol but what's life without a few vices? You notice the ringing the most when you've just finished an editing session, when you first take off those headphones and remember. It's strange you can forget something like that, especially with a reminder on the left side of your head. A horizontal sliver where the hair will never grow back, where it took thirteen stitches and a metal plate to sew you back up. Some people's tinnitus is temporary, the doctors told you with rehearsed voices, but every morning you wake up, you're pretty sure yours isn't going anywhere.

The studio is cold. The studio is *always* cold. You pay the heating bill on time and you never let the tank go below half-empty but there are too many spaces for the heat to fill. You find yourself zippering your hoodie even in the heart of August. The place is dark too. You've tried everything. The sets are professionally lit but once you step a foot out of bounds, it's like the shadows welcome you. It's like the sun has never visited this part of Massachusetts. You could move, of course, pack your bags and travel west. Between the channel's monetization and the Patreon subscribers, you make enough to relocate. The boys wouldn't mind. They want somewhere warmer. But the studio's monthly rent is a steal this far north, and who are you kidding? You'd never leave this place.

The coffee finishes brewing. You add one ice cube, then another, until it's tepid enough to drink. You're not in this for the taste but the temporary jolt to push you over the hump of exhaustion. It won't last. It never does. But you'll take what you can get.

As you're sipping, mulling over a third ice cube, you hear something over the ringing. A shifting sound from downstairs. The boys usually come up the fire escape and through the side entrance but the door sticks. The hinges have rusted from time and the elements.

Sometimes, when you open it just the right way, it sounds like screaming. But the sound downstairs is more like rummaging or scratching.

"Son of a bitch," you say, nearly spilling the coffee. You turn on every light in the studio. You don't see the intruder but you hear it. Every time you make your way to one corner, sure you've found it, the thing scurries in the other direction. You think it's a cat. You fear it's a raccoon. It's probably just trying to stay warm. This is the coldest winter on record, according to the local news station and *The Old Farmer's Almanac*. You wonder how the thing got in. You've seen no holes in the roof or walls but when you're desperate enough, when you have nothing to lose, you'll do anything to find a safe space.

You vow to the scurrying thing that its days are numbered. You'll try all the tricks. Traps and weapons and even animal control if it doesn't find a new place to hibernate. If it ruins any of the sets, there'll be hell to pay. This is your *life*. You work hard on something that seems so silly once it's uploaded to the general public, but neither they nor the intruder know what goes into it. The long hours and lack of sleep and even if it's a welcome distraction from why your ear won't stop ringing, it's still work. You tell it that between you two, you're the one putting the hours into this operation. The others help on-screen and with researching the films, but you're the one huddled in front of the computer in the dead of winter. You tell it many other things but after a while, you don't hear it scratching anymore.

Instead you sense someone standing just behind you.

Someone trying to keep quiet but doing a shit job.

You turn and almost spill your coffee when you see Ray and the boys standing in a group by one of the sets, just far enough from the lights that for a moment you're not entirely sure it's them.

"Everything okay?" Ray says. His eyes are wide, like he's dealing with a feral animal. Like he's dealing with the raccoon or cat or whatever the hell was just making a scene.

You shrug. "Yeah, sure. Just talking out loud."

Ray forces a smile and raises a six-pack. "You look like you could use one of these."

You chug the rest of your coffee, steal a bottle from the pack, and open it with one of the keys on your keychain.

You sip and belch and manage a laugh. The tension dissipates.

And you wonder, before you and the boys head upstairs, what you expected to see standing behind you if it wasn't them.

TWO

IT STARTED YEARS BACK, JUST after college. You, Todd, Eric, and Ray all moved home after your final semester. Four film school graduates, ready to light the industry ablaze, topple the studio system. Auteurs who would find a way to write, direct, produce, edit, distribute, and finance their own features without ever having to ask for favors.

You still can't believe it worked.

You lived within an hour of each other and after working part-time jobs at supermarkets and dying video rental stores, after realizing the blaze you envisioned was slow to spark, you got together one night in Todd's grandmother's basement with a handful of bad movies and no-name bottles of tequila.

Most of the movies came from Blockbuster's liquidation sale.

Late nineties direct-to-video garbage. Bad in the bad kind of way. But toward the end of the night, when the four of you were well past blitzed, you found a VHS at the bottom of the pile. The cardboard was sun-faded and the former rental shop had stuck a sticker on the center of the cover. And what a cover it was. A demonic cat, its mouth hanging open to reveal a smaller cat, even more sinister than the first.

The Uninvited.

"The hell is this?" you said, slurring, not sure if anyone heard you.

Eric had fallen asleep and Ray was trying to mix himself another drink, spilling most of it in the process.

"Found it at a yard sale," Todd answered. "There's a box of them somewhere. Thought that one looked the best."

"You thought right," you said, slipping the tape out of its sleeve and popping it into the VCR.

You talked amongst yourselves, cracking jokes at what might be in store, but by the ten-minute mark, you'd all grown silent. Todd sat inches from the screen, cross-legged on the floor like a child. Ray had finished making and drinking his cocktail, remnants dripping down his chin. And Eric had woken from his nap, more confused than the rest of you at the puppet on-screen, the cat vomiting up another cat. From there it was chaos and by the end of the night, you said, "Let's film it next time."

"Film what?" Todd said.

"Us."

"That's been done before. It's called *Mystery Science Theater.*"

You nodded but even then you knew it would be different. Your channel wouldn't just crack jokes, wouldn't just revel in the schlock. No, you'd grade on a curve. Poke fun when necessary but remind the viewers (assuming there'd be any) that movies take time and money and sometimes when you have neither, you come up with something beautiful.

The boys agreed, even if they thought you were full of shit.

The first video did well and the second did even better.

The third and fourth got mentions in some high-profile film blogs.

The fifth video went viral.

Soon you were sinking more time into the channel, until you didn't need that day job anymore. The viewership grew and so did the demand. You started renting studio space in an old mechanic's building on the outskirts of town, nothing around but abandoned factories and a sports bar that never seemed to open.

Videos six through twenty brought in thousands and eventually millions of views.

But it was video twenty-seven that changed things.

Not because Patton Oswalt and Simon Pegg retweeted you or because you landed your first public appearance at a convention.

Around the time you filmed video twenty-seven, you met Beth.

And now Beth is just a scar on the left side of your head.

THREE

"YOU FEELING OKAY?" RAY SAYS. He keeps his voice low so the others won't hear, as if the others aren't aware you're withering by the day. You've caught glimpses of yourself in the mirror and what you see looks like someone else. Someone who's lost too much weight despite a steady diet of Doritos and Mountain Dew. And don't forget the beer. Someone whose eyes are encased in dark circles the color of bruises, whose five o'clock shadow is usually closer to ten. Ray cares about you. You've known each other the longest. You met Todd and Eric in college, but you and Ray? You've been friends since middle school, bonded by a love of latex monster suits and over-the-top car chases.

"I'm fine," you say, listening above the ringing for any sign of the intruder.

You're in the kitchen, eating your third slice of pizza. The guy at the local sub shop cuts you a deal for ordering so often. Three pies for the price of two. You always opt for pepperoni while the others order vegetables. Your paper plate is stained with a river of orange grease and you wonder with each slice what the oil's doing to your insides. You often dream you've died and you're hovering over your body, watching the autopsy. When the surgeons slice open your belly, there's no blood or muscle. No organs of any kind. Only dough and cheese and marinara sauce.

Ray waits for the others to head into the screening room. He tells them you'll be right in. "Have you been sleeping here again?" he says.

You shrug. "Only sometimes. When it's two in the morning and you've been editing all day, what's the point in driving home?" You hold up your hands to delay his response. "I know what you're thinking. It's not as pathetic as it sounds. It's called time management." But what you really mean is you ought to break your lease and move into the studio full-time. Your apartment is just a mattress and a hand-me-down kitchen table that wobbles no matter how many folded electrical bills you place under the legs. Your upstairs neighbors can be heard fucking at all hours of the day. The food in the fridge has spoiled and sometimes you can't recall which side of the driveway is yours.

Ray doesn't push the subject but he places a hand on your shoulder and reminds you he's here. They're *all* here. But you don't need their pity. You're not looking for solutions. You're just trying to keep the channel going, trying to stay focused because when your mind wanders, sometimes you're afraid it won't come back.

You grab a fourth slice and a fifth beer and follow Ray into the screening room. The shelves stretch across every wall, a professional job that cost more than a month's rent. The curtains are black so as to block the sun. Sometimes you lose track of the days in here. It's like living in a fallout shelter, a bunker deep within the earth, guess-timating what horrible thing is taking place topside. If you stare long enough, you can find the remnants of the warehouse before you sunk thousands into the place. The ceiling tiles are warped from some ancient leak. You make a note to get it fixed, as if the fans will ever know.

You sit down on the couch. Each of you has their designated spots for the sake of continuity. An immense amount of editing needs to happen before the final videos are shared with the world and even though you're not filming tonight, even though this is just research and development, it would feel strange to sit anyplace else. The springs push against your lower back, like raking fingernails, but you don't mind.

"Okay," Todd says, standing. He always opens up with a speech, some secret society in the midst of a ritual. He likes the attention. On camera, he's the shyest of the group. He gets in some jokes now and then but he's hardly the life of the party. During research, though, it's like he's a leading man. You don't mind. Less work for you. "We've got three movies to get through tonight." He holds them up, two VHS tapes and a DVD. "Hopefully they're garbage, but *good* garbage."

You couldn't agree more. You've had three weeks of failure. Every now and then, you'll unearth a proverbial diamond in the rough, a movie that's actually decent, but those don't work for the channel. You need something bad but charming. Something that can be celebrated for its idiosyncrasies and odd choices. The worst thing a film can be is boring. Especially when your main source of income involves discussing them. The last three bad movie nights turned up nothing. Paint-by-numbers slashers and buddy cop flicks all seemingly shot in the same back alley. But tonight you've got a good feeling.

Todd holds up the first film. A generic action movie with a Rambo wannabee on the cover. He's holding a shotgun twice the size of his bulging arm. That's a good sign.

He holds up the second film. An *Alien* rip-off that promises "even more terror" but probably shows the creature for all of thirty seconds. You're less enthusiastic for this one.

He holds up the third film, the one in the DVD case, and claims you've been waiting for this day. The cover looks as though it's been printed on someone's inkjet circa 1997. The scanlines slice through the image and the quality is so poor you're not sure what you're looking at. The others turn their heads at an angle, trying to piece the puzzle together. It's a Rorschach test and none of you is coming up with anything.

"Ladies and gentlemen," Todd says, asking for a drum roll. You all slap your hands against your knees and even though you're jaded, even though you've seen more cinematic filth than any one person should, you can't help but giggle.

"Allow me to introduce you to a film each of us has been after for nearly a decade, one so notorious we still can't believe we haven't tracked down a copy. We've tried eBay and Amazon and sites that have probably put us on the FBI watchlist. We've put out want ads and asked around at conventions, but each time we've come up empty handed. For a hot minute there, we thought this thing didn't exist. But I'm here tonight to prove us wrong. What I hold in my hands is a bootleg of a bootleg. It might look like shit but it's priceless in my book."

"Get on with it," Eric says. He's stopped his drum roll.

"*Creepies*," Todd says. "An actual real-life copy of motherfucking *Creepies*."

The room grows quiet and the ringing floods your ears. You can hear your own heartbeat when it pumps fast enough and right now it's on overdrive.

"Gimme that," you say, reaching out.

Todd tosses it. "See for yourself."

It lands on the coffee table, almost knocking over your beer in the process. You pick it up but, this close, the image isn't any clearer. You suppose those could be the (in)famous mini-monsters you've read about on message boards and sub-Reddits, but the longer you stare, you wonder if they're something else. The back-cover copy isn't any better. The words are so faded they've become symbols. Hieroglyphics neither of you has the talent to interpret.

Someone's left behind a brown ring in the upper right-hand corner, a coffee mug's imprint. You wonder who took the time to make bootlegs of a film so obscure many people assume it's just a rumor. And you wonder, too, who owns the original copy. Patient zero, so to speak.

You open the case but the disk has no label, just a silver surface reflecting your tired eyes. Your pupils seem dilated, like the night your ear started ringing and never stopped, but you chalk it up to a trick of the light. Someone has written the title—*Creepies*—in a strange font. None of the letters match up, as if each was scribbled by a different hand.

Ray snatches it away before you can study it any longer. You can't help but think you would've never let go on your own accord, that if no one else had been in the screening room, you would've spent days studying those mismatching letters.

Ray shrugs. "Could be a fake."

"Or it could be the real thing," Todd says. He turns to Eric.

Eric's the fact machine of the group. Wanna know a director's pseudonym? Ask Eric. Year of a film's release? Ask Eric. Wanna learn some minute detail from a film's production? Eric's on it. He provides much of the meat and potatoes for the videos. You've thought about paying him more for his troubles but if the other two caught on, things could get ugly. Besides, not much is known about *Creepies*, which has only added to its internet lore.

"What do you think?" Todd says to Eric. "Team maybe or team maybe not?"

Eric turns the DVD case like he's trying to solve an optical illusion. "I plead the fifth for now."

"That's two for team maybe not," Todd says.

"I said 'I plead the fifth.'"

"Same difference." Todd points to you. "How about a tie?"

You don't want to let them down. The suspense is something palpable. Why not play along? You lower your voice for dramatic effect. "I want to believe."

"Two and two," Todd says as he places the case at the bottom of the pile.

FOUR

THERE ARE THOUSANDS OF FILMS that never made it to DVD, much less Blu-ray.

In the eighties and nineties, during the height of the video boom, the market was flooded with content. Now, with streaming, the playing field has been leveled, but back then, the video stores gave Netflix and Hulu a run for their money, even if neither existed yet. Suddenly, smaller production companies were able to crank out films on the cheap. Many fly-by-night operations took advantage of rental stores and most of them died a quick and quiet death. Still, plenty of production houses flourished by releasing films from hack screenwriters and directors, with lurid covers of demons tearing victims limb from limb or Conan-esque barbarians holding swords toward starry skies. And don't forget the skin. Sex sells, always and forever, and never was that more apparent than the video boom. If you wanted to market your movie to adults, you needed a scantily clad woman somewhere on the cover, even if they weren't in your film and even if your female lead was closer to retirement age. A far cry from today's PC culture, but things were different then and you've got to view films with a lens, no matter how sleazy.

And there's nothing wrong with a little sleaze.

Some titles from this era are so obscure and sought after that collectors fork over thousands for a copy. *Creepies* is in this camp. A fourth-rate *Gremlins*, so the story goes. Not good enough to touch *Critters* or *Ghoulies* or even *Munchies*. The synopsis, depending on which forum you choose to believe, is your standard fare—at least at first. Five friends throw a party in an abandoned mansion, except it's not really abandoned. The former owner, one Hector Taffey, was into some strange shit. Voodoo, witchcraft—you name it. Messed around with ancient texts, learned to speak in tongues long dead, and managed to summon a handful of puppy-sized demons. If it sounds like a tired concept, you're right, but it's the supposed execution that sets *Creepies* apart from other Z-grade creature features of the time.

That and its troubled production.

If the stills are to be believed, the creature effects are quite impressive. The puppets have several points of articulation. Their eyes move in four directions and the mouths look to be more lifelike than Gizmo himself. The effects coordinator, whose name is listed as Harry Katz (a pseudonym, no doubt), was said to be a well-known artist who only did the film as a favor. Because of this, the production value is much higher than it has any right to be.

At least for the first half.

Because, you see, *Creepies* is really two movies. The first is the pint-sized puppet portion, but when the producers were less than enthused by the dailies, they fired the director and hired someone who is, by all accounts, unnamed. The cast and crew quit the production in protest. Director number one treated them well, let them improvise, and allowed them to stay for free in the shooting location.

After the first crew hit the road, a second was brought in and so began the quest to finish the movie. Except the unnamed director, sometimes referred to as Mr. C, didn't seem to understand the film he was making. His portion of *Creepies* is experimental, to put it lightly. Gone are the puppets and the house itself appears different. The walls change color by the shot and the rooms always seem off. There's one shot in which a chair appears on the ceiling, some dark shape sitting upside down in defiance of gravity.

It's because of this reputation *Creepies* has earned its mythical status and even though you believe most of it's probably bullshit, it's still fun to play along.

You have vague memories of grasping the tape in your local rental shop, no older than seven or eight, staring at the cover and thinking the puppets were stupid, yet you could never get them out of your mind. They came to you at odd times. When you were taking math quizzes or about to finish your paper route. But whenever you returned to the shop, it was always out of stock. You played this song and dance for years, until the business went under. By then, you'd all but forgotten the tape.

But now, with a possible replica resting on the coffee table, next to the junk food brought out in anticipation of the night's festivities, it's like the opposite is true.

You may have forgotten *Creepies* but *Creepies* remembers you.

FIVE

THE ACTION FILM ISN'T HALF bad. There's some unforgivable ADR and everyone's gun seems to run on infinite ammo, but that's all par for the B-movie course. You write notes for each scene, bullet points (so to speak) to discuss for the video. The film makes the cut by the end of its eighty-minute runtime. You maintain a three-page rule. If you can write three pages of material, jokes, and talking points, it's good enough for the channel. Sometimes you can already see the video in your mind, where you'll cut to clips or show the same kill over and over for comedic effect. Sometimes you do this with your life too. Like back in the kitchen, when Ray was trying to console you. You wish you could cut past that part. And with your intruder from earlier. You'd like to fast forward to when you find the thing. But if you're being honest, if you could choose one edit in your life, you'd delete the scene just before the crash, because then you wouldn't have a bald spot or a ringing ear and Beth could laugh along with the group.

The *Alien* rip-off's up next. Pretzel and chip crumbs litter the floor. By now, everyone's well on their way to intoxicated. They're laughing louder and talking over the dialogue. You can't hear half the lines. It doesn't matter. You know a *bad* film when you see one. And this one is putrid. The lighting is nearly non-existent. You can hardly see the characters or their motorcycle helmets, painted with silver swirls to pass as futuristic. The same industrial hallways are used for every shot and no one's fooled by the big reveal. The director didn't choose to hide the creature in shadows, hoping your mind would fill in the gaps. The suit is garbage and not in a good way. A gorilla Halloween costume with some extra flare. You share a few chuckles and oh-shit moments but for the most part, it's a lost cause. Barely one page of notes.

Last film of the night.

Creepies, you're up.

Todd takes his time with it, humming the theme to *The Twilight Zone* and spinning the DVD case like you're about to engage in group hypnosis. He pops the disc out. Even from across the room you can see those strange letters. Todd slides the disc into the DVD player and turns the television to max volume. You want to tell him to turn it down but everyone's having a good time. The doctors have warned that exposure to loud sounds could make your tinnitus worse. They say you have a predisposition to hearing loss. You've always thought that was a strange word for it: predisposition. What you have is a grayish worm-like scar and a section of your skull that took months to heal properly. They say concerts and DJs are the most dangerous, followed closely by power tools and lawn mowers, but you have to wonder what else is too loud. Could the television be causing more damage?

You realize the group has stopped talking and laughing and even drinking.

The title card appears on-screen in blood-dripping letters.

Creepies.

No previews or menu. One moment the screen's black, then you're thrust into a film you've been chasing since boyhood. It's real. You can't believe it's real. After a quick prologue of Hector Taffey messing with the black arts, there's a wide shot of a deserted road, crooked cornstalks sprouting on either side. In the distance two headlights approach the camera. The shot lingers, takes its time setting the mood. The ominous score, with its out-there time signature, is the cherry on top. It's like Carpenter if he dropped acid. The headlights draw closer until the scene cuts to the interior of the car.

It's your typical cast of unlikeables, everyone dressed to fit a different clique. There's the jock, with his high school football jacket, and the punk, with his nose ring connected by a silver chain to his eyebrow ring. Then there's the stoner, smoking a joint the size of your index finger and giggling at everything. And who could forget the girls? You've got your slut—two of them to be precise—and the quiet, virginal next-door-neighbor that would be the final girl if the film didn't shift gears at the forty-five-minute mark. She might've been the last one standing, but you'll never know if she made it. It bothers you, her story unfinished, like she's still running through the same rooms and screaming for help.

The characters arrive at the mansion and kill the engine. Jock's been driving, complaining how bored he is. He steps out and finishes off his road soda, crushes it against his forehead and tosses it into the weeds. We cut to a POV shot of something low to the ground. Something roughly the size of a puppet creature. It doesn't appreciate litter on its home turf and shows as much with a deep grunt.

Cut back to the kids. Jock's straining to hear.

"What was that?" he says.

"What was what?" Punk says. He rolls his eyes. "Let's get moving, okay? Place gives me the creeps."

"Thought I heard something," Jock says.

Stoner pats him on the back. "And you said *I* was the paranoid one. Come on, let's do this." He's carrying a boombox in one hand and a Ziploc overflowing with weed in the other, though it looks more like oregano and catnip.

The group banters for another minute before they step into the house. It's your standard haunted-mansion fare. Cobwebs in the corners. Paint peeling from the walls like dead skin. They walk over loose floorboards, every member of the group oblivious to the pentagram scratched into the hallway wall. They wind up in the living room, where there's nothing but a couch, a table, and soot-stained fireplace. Stoner sets down the supplies.

Slut One and Slut Two are carrying the cooler, arguing who's going to sleep with who. They crack open a few cold ones. That's when the music starts and the dancing ensues. It's painfully awkward. Their moves don't sync up with the generic synth pop track. You scrawl several notes, trying to keep up with your observations. This scene is gold. One page down.

The music cuts when the group hears a sound deep within the house. Something shifting, scratching, not unlike your intruder in the studio. They decide to investigate. The smartest plan of action, Stoner informs them, is to split up on their own. They can cover more ground that way. Final Girl begs to differ but no one's listening to her.

For the next thirty-five minutes, you're treated to kill after kill, all of them well staged and executed. The blood is bright red, a la *Dawn of the Dead* or *Suspiria*, and it gives the film a sort of hyper-realism. The gore is something to admire. You'll be pausing and observing plenty while editing. You've heard that Harry Katz, whoever he may actually be, went on to win an Oscar and you can see why. If *Creepies* was widely available, it would be a classic. Revered along the same lines as *Basket Case*. It's got all the right ingredients and it's meant to be watched with a crowd, hence the laughter and Ray choking on his cheese curls. Stoner's pinned down on a stone slab, a sacrificial altar in the basement, while the puppets are going to town on him. Blood is not just flowing but spurting, as if he's been hiding a geyser in his abdomen.

You can't remember the last time you enjoyed a film like this.

Watching so much trash has hardened you. Not much surprises you anymore but this—this is next level. It makes you remember why you started the channel. A way to cope with life's troubles, and even if those troubles have intensified over the years, this is proof of what corn syrup and latex can do if you allow it.

You're scribbling notes. Two pages. Three. Eight and nine and ten, and you're about to tell the boys to pause so you can grab another beer and take a leak when the film transitions into its second half.

Stoner's screams are cut short. There's a shot of his face, eyes bulging while the puppets laugh and snicker and then everything fades to black. Except there's something *in* the blackness. Something vaguely lighter than the rest of the shadows. The camera focuses slowly and you see that it's the pentagram from the front hallway. It seems to glow green now, the color of toxic sludge. The soundtrack has changed as well. Carpenter worship has given way to ambient drones. To your knowledge, only one composer was used for the film but it's hard to imagine they're the same person. It doesn't sound like music at all but a droning gust of wind so strong you feel it in the studio.

Someone's just starting to complain about the lingering shot—you're not sure who since you can't quite hear them over the drone—when the camera pans down the hall and into the living room. A POV shot the approximate height of a person. It studies the room. The table and cooler and boombox are gone. Above the droning is something like breathing. It's not an original concept.

Black-gloved killers did the same in giallo films and Michael Myers led an army of masked slashers through the same set-up years before *Creepies*. But this feels different, like whoever's eyes you're supposed to be looking through aren't just interested in stalking prey.

The camera studies the fireplace. It wasn't lit before but now there's a small flame sputtering to life, letting off black smoke you can almost smell. The shot shifts toward the ceiling where you see the upside-down chair and its infamous upside-down inhabitant. The lighting is so poor you're not sure if the shadow is staring toward the camera or away, though you hope it's the latter.

Hard cut to the stairs, the POV shot walking toward the many bedrooms, one of which was the puppets' lair in the previous film. You weren't prepared for just how jarring the transition would be. By the looks of it, neither was the group. You've all done your research but the forums didn't do *Creepies* justice. It's no wonder why the film fell into obscurity. It takes a special kind of fan to watch this sort of thing. You think about telling the boys to shut it off. There's already more than enough material. But opening your mouth seems like a chore. Even blinking takes effort. Better to sit back and let the rest play out. What's the worst that could happen?

The camera takes its time with the hall, each door creaking open slowly, though you never see a hand turning the knobs. Every room is empty save for the last. You think there's something wrong with the transfer. It's a bootleg after all, a copy of a copy, but the quality doesn't account for the way the far wall ripples, like it's not wood but water. The camera zooms. You swear there's something beneath the surface, reaching toward the camera, toward the screen, toward the group. But the strange part is you never *see* it, only sense it.

You're about to ask if the others feel it too when your vision erupts into a burst of static, like snow on a television. You blink. The screening room lights turn on.

The screen has gone black. No closing credits or music. No static. Ray stands near the light switch. His eyes are reddened and swollen, as though he's just emerged from a coma.

"What happened?" you say.

"I was going to ask you the same thing," he says.

"What do you mean 'what happened?'" Eric says. "Movie's over." He reaches for a pretzel but stops halfway, arm hovering like it might be a trap. "The movie *is* over, right?"

You shrug, point to the screen.

Todd stretches and yawns. "We fell asleep, that's all." He looks at his watch. "No wonder. It's fucking three a.m."

"No way," Ray says as you check your phones and confirm Todd's on the money. "It was barely eleven last time I checked."

"*Was*," Todd says, "but like I said, we dozed off. Not the first time."

You nod your head *yes*, like you believe him. You don't remember closing your eyes or dreaming and you certainly don't remember waking up. It's like there's a gap, some missing piece of information, and you're close to remembering, yet part of you doesn't want to.

"We can finish watching while we film," Eric says. "Even if the rest is boring, we've got the puppets. We can work with that, yeah?"

You shrug *sure*. It'll seem more natural if you're watching for the first time on camera. You tell them you'll set everything up for tomorrow night. Usually you choose three films per episode but even though the *Alien* rip-off was pure garbage, you've got enough to talk about between the action flick and *Creepies*, which is really two films anyway, even if none of you remembers the second one.

Everyone stretches and wishes each other a good night. Todd was going to be the designated driver but they all seem half-drunk. Eric calls an Uber while Ray follows you back into the kitchen to help clean up. You want to ask him how he feels, if he's also suspicious you didn't just fall asleep, but he cuts you off with another pity plea.

"You want to crash at my place?" he says, even though it's ten minutes farther than your apartment.

You wave him off. "I'll make another cup of coffee, work on the episode for an hour, then I'll be good to drive."

"You sure?"

"Positive." You scratch at your scar.

Sometimes it itches when you lie.

SIX

YOU DO MAKE COFFEE, DOUBLE brew it for extra caffeine, and you do work on the episode, an hour turning into three, but you don't leave the studio. There's a sink in the bathroom and you keep an overnight—now *every* night—stockpile of supplies. Soap and shampoo and deodorant. You use the mirror and faucet to make yourself look halfway decent even if you won't be going anywhere today. The weather promises record-breaking low temperatures and stepping outside seems absurd. Your car's battery isn't doing so well and the mechanic warned it would give you trouble on the first real day of the winter. It's been dormant in the lot for, what, three days now? You can turn that key all you want but the engine's got other plans.

You pour water over your head, squirt shampoo into your palm.

Your hair's getting long but you don't mind. Helps to cover the scar. You dry off with a towel that's seen better days and hide the supplies under the sink, behind extra rolls of toilet paper. You don't need Ray giving you any more lectures, even if he means well. You think about shaving but not for long. You always wanted to grow a beard. Beth said you looked like someone else when you didn't shave, a stranger she couldn't place, and for that reason you kept your cheeks baby smooth. Now it makes no difference.

You shut the faucet off and the ringing returns. It's not as loud as it could be. Mornings are usually the best. The more the day passes, the louder the ringing. It tends to change pitch through the hours, and just when you start to get used to one tone, it reminds you there are infinite possibilities. The doctors offered you an in-ear white noise machine, a small contraption resembling a hearing aid. It transmits frequencies to cancel out the ringing, but that's just re-placing one sound with another.

You turn on the Bluetooth speaker and set your film score playlist to random. There are nearly five hundred tracks, everything from *Gone with the Wind* to *Candyman*. You often imagine yourself on-screen while a composer adjusts his tempos. But if that were true, if your life were just a bad movie, you wish there was a punch-line, some comedic relief. The thought chills you. You don't like not being in control, especially after what happened—or didn't—in the screening room last night.

You make breakfast, if you call freezer-burnt Pizza Rolls break-fast. You sit at your small kitchen table, not wincing at the clash in flavors since you don't notice the taste to begin with. The video's just about done. One more watch-through for quality assurance and you should be ready to hit *upload*. You stand to clean off your plate when you hear the scratching over the playlist.

You note the time—nine-thirty-seven—and wonder if it's on some sort of schedule. At first you jog but then you think about keeping surprise on your side. Again you wonder how it got in but mice are amazing creatures, able to squeeze through cracks a third the size of their body. There are traps around here somewhere, just-in-case supplies you purchased when you first rented the space. With your luck, they'd only stun the thing and you'd hear it scratching in less steady patterns. The one thing that could drive you closer to crazy.

You head downstairs into the storage space, past the sets. You listen. It's there. The scratching is there, but it's faint. And from which direction? You stare toward the bay door, where the former owners brought cars in and out. You shake your head. The side door then. There's a small gap where it meets the concrete. You take one step in that direction and the noise fades. Not there either. It's got to be near the back door. There's a pile of old props you've been meaning to purge. The little bastard probably made himself a nest beneath the junk and who knows if there aren't more where that came from. You crouch, reach for one of the boxes, and just as you're ready to flip it, you realize you're wrong again. The sound isn't coming from the junk or the doors or any of the walls, for that matter. You look down.

The sound is coming from beneath you.

But that's not possible, right? Mice can't dig through something so solid. A hole in the foundation? A tiny tunnel that leads in and out? You kneel down and you're sure of it now. The scratching grows louder as you place your ringing ear against the cold concrete. It sounds steady, like whatever's working at the other side has been practicing. It's not giving up until it breaks through. But how long would that take, for something so small, so determined, to claw its way through a surface meant to withstand thousands of tons?

And what would something that determined do once it broke free?

~

You clean the kitchen and the screening room, do some categorizing of the recently donated movies. Take care of some emails and YouTube comments. Check the Patreon page. Aside from the video, none of these is urgent but you're not doing them to be productive.

Creepies is still in the DVD player, the homemade case on the table with its coffee ring from whoever copied it. You think again of the lost time, what you tried to convince yourself was exhaustion and a shared nap, and you wonder: do they know? Did the owner know what it would do to whoever watched? You pause the sound-track playlist and sit on the couch, in your favorite spot, and decide to watch the second half in its entirety. It'll be good to know what you're in for, gauge the beats and ticks and figure out if it's worth filming at all.

You press *play* and the DVD begins around the halfway mark. You don't remember setting a bookmark for the scene where Stoner is getting ripped apart, the exact spot where, seconds later, you're thrust into that jarring POV shot. Ray or Todd or Eric must have done it while you weren't looking. You watch the camera walk down the hall, quick pause on the pentagram, then the living room, then upstairs through the bedrooms where the camera zooms toward that far wall. That *rippling* wall. You're not tired this time. No more than usual anyway. You keep your eyes wide, don't even consider blinking, as the shot gets closer to the wood paneling that's more like water with a slight metallic tint. That must be it. There was a hidden cut and what you're seeing is a pool with some prop beneath the surface, a simple scare tactic and you're ready for it to emerge. Like before, you're certain it's moments away from the big reveal. So certain, it's like you're there.

Is that hair? Long hair slowly revealing itself? And are those eyes? Closed eyes that could open at any moment? And a small button nose that looks familiar, like you've studied it, like you've kissed it before turning in for the night? And those lips, those full lips that many people pay good money for. You know them when you see them because you see them in your dreams, and when you close your eyes for too long, but you won't do that now, because one more moment, a single frame, and you'll be sure of what you already know. That's Beth in there, in the water.

It's Beth.

SEVEN

YOU CALL RAY FIRST BECAUSE of course you do. Todd and Eric will think you're crazy, but Ray's always been open minded. As kids, you used to sneak out during sleepovers and head for the woods. You'd break out the flashlight and whichever book of supposed true stories you'd taken from the library that week. By day, the tales seemed far-fetched, but among the chirping crickets and whatever rustled the leaves, far-fetched took on a different meaning. One of you would hold the light under their chin, campfire style, and you'd read a passage at random. Sometimes the stories were heavy hitters. Bigfoot and Mothman and other grade-A cryptids, while others were more obscure, limited to particular regions of the country and world.

Every town's got its ghosts.

So do you.

Which is why you're blocking your ringing ear with one finger and telling Ray to fucking pick up already until he finally does.

"What's wrong?" he says, mostly because you don't call him these days. Not unless it's bad news. And this certainly counts as bad adjacent.

"Nothing," you say, when what you mean is *everything*. "Something came up. I need you to stop by."

Ray sighs on the other end. It sounds like static to your good ear. "I just cooked dinner, man. Alyssa will have my balls if I cut out early."

"Just woof it down and tell her you're running out for roses or something. It's important."

Before he can object, you hang up and head to the kitchen for more coffee. This time, you skip the ice cube because there's something calming as the molten liquid travels down your insides, reminds you you're alive and awake. Because otherwise, you'd be forgiven for mistaking this for a dream. You think about eating and then think better of it. Your stomach's filled with acid and the thought of food isn't helping matters. From here, you can see a sliver of the screening room and the television. The image is paused in the same location, the still frame of Beth as she emerges from the silver liquid. Her face appears pixelated. What should be a clear shot of her drenched cheeks winds up looking scrambled when it's frozen. You tried it a couple times before calling Ray, playing and pausing and repeating the process. Her eyes have that haunted-house-painting effect, the one where they follow your every move.

"You're not real," you call from the kitchen. "You can't be."

Your furry little intruder starts scratching again. It sounds closer somehow, even though you're one floor removed.

You step back into the screening room and there's someone else there. Someone sitting on the sofa and watching you. For just a moment, a second so small, it may as well have never happened, that person is Stoner, his abdomen carved up like Thanksgiving came early, but when you shake your head it's Ray telling you to hurry up already.

"How the hell'd you get here this quick?" you say, heading for the remote. "You take your dinner to go?"

"So quick?" Ray says, pausing for a punchline. When he doesn't receive one, he breaks out his cell. "You called me two hours ago."

"Bullshit," you say. There's no way you could've paced the kitchen for that long. Lucky for you, there's a litmus test right there in your hand, the coffee that's no doubt still scalding. You sip it, ready for the burn, only to find it two steps below tepid.

"Can we just get this over with?" Ray says. "Alyssa thinks I'm getting gas."

"Sure," you say, setting down the coffee, trying not to think about the lost time. You point to the screen, which seems even more scrambled now. "Tell me what you see."

Ray squints. "A girl in a bathtub?" he says.

You groan. "Let me rewind," which you do, right up to the point where the chair is hovering upside down just before the POV shot begins.

"*Creepies*," Ray says. At least he's paying attention. "I thought we were waiting to finish it."

"So did I," you say, telling him to keep it down, to wait for it, and there she is. There's Beth emerging from the watery wall. You pause again and the image grows splotchy, abstract. "Remind you of anyone?"

Ray shrugs but his eyes tell a different story. They were tired slits moments ago but now they're wide craters. He knows where this is headed even before you tell him.

"It's her," you say. "It's Beth."

Ray's face betrays the annoyance he must feel. After all, it's been three years since the crash. If you were him, you'd get tired of you too. "It does kind of look like her. But you don't really think." He stops it there, doesn't bother with an ellipsis.

"I do think," you say. You rewind and show him once more for good measure. "She told me she'd been in a couple movies. Low-budget stuff. But she never spilled the specifics. Too embarrassing, she said, like embarrassing isn't my expertise."

"The timing doesn't work," Ray says. "This is movie is, what, thirty-five years old? So is Beth. She would've still been on the bottle."

"I know it sounds crazy." You don't bother with the rest, how you plan to track down whoever donated the DVD. Even if they don't have answers, they might know someone who does.

"You're tired," Ray says, standing and planting a hand on your shoulder. "I don't blame you for making connections where there aren't any. It looks like her. I'll give you that much. But you know, on some level, it isn't. Right?"

"We'll see," you say, staring at the screen, at the shimmering girl who stares back.

~

You promise Ray you won't do anything stupid, like spend the rest of the evening combing through the trash.

Let's be honest, you've never been good at promises.

Which is why you're tearing open garbage bags and searching for bubble-wrapped envelopes. Like the editing (and the posting and the comments and don't even get you started), you handle most of the viewer donations. The channel has enough fans and Patreon supporters to supply you with eons of trash cinema. A large portion of the movies are doubles but you've still discovered hundreds of films you wouldn't have otherwise. Someone donated *Creepies*. You've just got to find out who. Todd assists you sometimes, which is why he got to it first. You could call him, but chances are he'll pretend it just appeared. He loves the air of mystery behind *Creepies*. For him, it's a game. For you, it's something else.

What you find are twenty-two torn-open packages, one of which could've housed *Creepies* before Todd extracted it. You hold the case up to the envelopes. At least half are too skinny, which tells you those held VHS tapes, not a DVD. If memory serves, you're able to rule out another eight you remember opening yourself. That leaves three possibilities but the envelopes themselves aren't exactly clues.

You'll have to contact all three fans. At least that's what you think until you notice the stain on the back of the farthest emptied package. You slide it over. This close, the splotch looks not unlike a ring of coffee. The same ring of coffee that's on the *Creepies* label itself. It must be a logo of some sort. You pay close attention to the name of the sender, one Matt Beaumont. Doesn't ring a bell but you do some Googling anyway. And you're glad you did. Turns out Mr. Beaumont runs a company called Garbage Films Preservation Project, GFPP for short. His business model is all about preserving movies that have never made it to any format post-VHS. That's something you can get behind, especially if *Creepies* is part of his catalogue. You scroll through the list of titles but come up empty.

"Shit," you say to your computer in the editing suite, and whatever's been scratching at the wall scratches again in response.

A search of their Facebook profile and Instagram page tells you they're at a horror convention this weekend, located fifty miles west, in central Massachusetts. The event, SpookyCon, will be open through noon tomorrow. You've done plenty of cons yourself, especially when the channel first started. Back then, it was necessary to get your name out there. These days, you've got the privilege of hanging tight more often, but this is the perfect opportunity to dive back into the circuit, especially to have a chat with GFPP.

The venue, a college hockey/basketball arena, opens for business at nine a.m. That gives you just enough time for a few hours of shut-eye. But who're you kidding? Sleep's not in the cards tonight.

Besides, it might take that long just to warm the car up.

EIGHT

AT THIS TIME OF MORNING, I-95 is mostly barren, unless you count the eighteen-wheelers and the deer carcasses animal control hasn't gotten around to. There's a long drive ahead of you, with only highway to entertain. Luckily you've got your playlist and a rest stop every twenty or so miles. You pull off at the nearest one and ask the clerk to point you in the direction of the coffee station. You opt for the largest cup they offer, which is plastic and meant for the soda machine, but what's life without a little anarchy? You choose iced coffee this time, so as not to melt said plastic.

The cashier gives you a suspicious glance as she rings you out. "Little early for soda, isn't it?"

"Five o'clock somewhere," you tell her.

Outside, in the cold that's only gotten colder, your fingertips don't take kindly to the frigid cup. You were smart to leave the engine running, but if this were one of a thousand slashers, that might be inviting trouble. You've never been one for superstition but, given what's brought you on the road today, you check the backseat just to be safe. It's empty save for the ancient discarded fast-food bags.

You pull back onto the road, sipping coffee that tastes like battery acid and listening to the score to *Bram Stoker's Dracula*, orchestral sweeps and swells to keep away the ringing in your ear and any unwanted thoughts, but the problem with the latter is they always win.

Beth it is.

The weird thing about Beth is you don't remember meeting her.

You might've been bowling with the boys or maybe it was that midnight screening of *The Shining* in Bass Falls. She used to work the concession stand before they tore it down to build a Target. After that came her supposed brief run as a failed actress. You can't recall the moment you first saw her. You know the year and roughly the month but your mind has a difficult time computing what it was like before her. Before Beth. Some coping mechanism probably. Because if you sat back and really thought about it, considered how little of your life Beth occupied, the ringing and *Creepies* would be the least of your worries.

You asked her once, both of you half-asleep on the couch while an old episode of the *X-Files* played on mute. The living room was mostly shadows and squinting at the screen stung your eyes.

"Do you remember how we met?" you said.

She yawned and shifted all her weight to your outstretched arm, which swarmed with pins and needles, but you didn't dare speak up. Besides, it grew numb eventually. "Huh?"

"The first time we met. Was it bowling or something? The movies maybe?"

She opened one eye, managed to roll it. "You really don't remember?"

You shrugged and decided to change the subject. But she wouldn't let it go. She sat up, cross-legged, and teased you. "You think it was a bowling alley?"

"That or the movies."

She shook her head.

"A bar?"

"Getting warmer."

"I give up."

You thought she'd be mad but for some reason she smiled, like she found your poor memory funny. But you weren't laughing. You and Beth, what you added up to, it was more important than any movie you'd ever seen. More important than the channel even if the fans had begun to like her the most. She was a breath of fresh air, they said. A welcome reprieve from excess masculinity, according to some of the comments.

"Tell you what," she said, "if you don't remember by your thirtieth birthday, I'll remind you. That'll be your present. Maybe a six-pack if you're lucky. I'd buy you a movie but you seem to own them all."

You were twenty-five then, on the couch, Mulder and Scully silently arguing about a manitou. You wanted to say you couldn't wait that long but she was smiling with those two deep dimples and getting up for a midnight soda. And you read between her lines, deduced that five years was a long time from then. It sounded like she planned on sticking around.

But you're not smiling now because now there's no promise to fill in the details later. No *X-Files* or midnight soda and there sure as hell aren't any dimples.

You can tell yourself it was bowling, that Beth was playing tricks, and you can tell yourself *Creepies* is just two regular movies stitched together, but the rest of you isn't buying it. The rest of you knows an omen when you see it.

NINE

IN THE DISTANCE, THE CONVENTION venue comes
into view. At this hour, the city is dark and empty, save for the occasional cop car and drug dealer. The street is littered with potholes
in the wake of the most recent snowstorm. You do your best to
swerve around them. Last thing you need is a flat tire *and* an ailing
battery. You find the venue's parking lot across the street, next to a
closed-down McDonald's, mostly used for graffiti these days. The
Sunday fee is fifteen dollars. A bargain according to the toothless
attendant. You pay up and back into the closest space, which offers
a view of the venue's side entrance. Above the door is a poster for a
hockey team that's lost on you. Sports were never your thing. Seems
like a lot of effort.

You stay like that for two hours, until the sky lightens to a pale gray and the line for admission begins to form. It's starting to drizzle out there. You wish you'd brought an umbrella but, like sports, planning ahead has never been in your skill set. The line's only six fans deep, each of them excited to fork over hard-earned money for knock-off memorabilia and bootleg shirts. Not that you're judging. You've got piles of the stuff back at the studio. If you had more time, you'd gladly sift through posters and action figures but you've got GFPP on the mind.

Eventually, the doors open and you pay an additional twenty dollars to gain entry to the vendor floor. The place is a ghost town, so to speak, and will likely stay that way. Sundays are the witching hour of conventions. By then, the vendors and most of the full-weekend-attendees are too hungover to be bothered. If the latter do make it to the floor, they shuffle through the rows like the undead. If you're looking for a deal, though, Sundays are a proverbial gold mine. Vendors have high hopes on Friday evening but two days later, there's no way in hell they want to lug everything back. They usually slash prices and if you're good at bartering, you might find the deal of the century.

You head for the bathrooms first because it was a long drive. You should fix your hair, splash some water on that face of yours. You want to make a good impression after all. Someone took the time to smash a vertical crack into the mirror and thus far, it's gone unfixed. You tell your bisected reflection you've got this. Today is the day you find answers. From the closest stall, someone groans for you to shut the fuck up. You can practically feel the headache from here.

"Sorry about that," you say. "Go back to sleep."

Back on the floor, your next stop is the food window in the corner. This early, all they're serving is coffee and soggy breakfast sandwiches, both of which will do just fine. Convention cuisine is always a gamble but you're a junk food veteran. You can handle the sodium and the grease. You devour the sandwich in three bites and nurse the coffee while you take your first lap around the dealer room. Everyone's still getting set up, looking as tired as you feel.

On the far side of the floor is the roped-off celebrity area. You've never liked the way it reminds you of a zoo, each animal in their cage while the general public observes them from a safe distance. You notice some familiar faces, scream queens and unmasked killers. Sure, their careers may not have thrived in the traditional sense, but each has their own dedicated fan base. And the pay for convention appearances is nothing to snicker at. Take thirty dollars for a head shot, multiply it by hundreds or even thousands, and you've got a decent chunk of change.

Closer by are the vendors. You head that way and hope for the best. As they pull blankets from their merch like mid-trick magicians, you spot trinkets and head shots and rare tapes but none as rare as *Creepies*.

Speaking of which, there's a corner table, surrounded by tall stacks of front-facing DVDs with poorly printed covers. The video-rental-store theme gives you a severe case of the warm fuzzies. Above the closest rack is a neon sign that sputters to life: GFPP.

Target acquired.

You make your way down the aisle, give the guy—Matt, presumably—counting ones and tens a minute to finish up, then step behind the only other customer, a green-haired girl with a Michael Myers shoulder tattoo. She asks Matt if he's ever seen *Halloween*. He's trying his best not to roll his eyes. It's something fanatics are guilty of far too often. You assume everyone else in the world has seen every deep cut, every piece of cult cinema, and when you're reminded that's not the case, you turn up your nose like some professor with tenure. You're not saying it's right. You're just saying it happens. But Matt makes a quick recovery and tells the girl yeah, he's seen it. About a million times, and it changed his life. They chat for a few more minutes before she starts perusing the aisles. You're next.

"Hey, man," Matt says without looking up from his phone. "Be right with you." This close, you notice the *Chopping Mall* tattoo on his forearm. His shaved head is covered with a Freddy-branded baseball cap. He's good people.

"Sure," you say, already reaching into your pocket.

Matt finishes texting and finally looks up. Since he's a fan, he recognizes you right way. "Holy shit. You're . . ."

You nod. "Sure am. Cool stuff you got here." You point to the movies, none of which are entirely legal. It's not like GFPP has secured the rights to these titles. This isn't a boutique film label. This is more of a gray-market operation. But you're not FBI. You're just here to talk.

"Thanks, man," Matt says, fidgeting now. It still blows your B-movie mind that someone can think of you as famous. Don't they know you're a thirty-something who hovers over his computer most days, listening to soundtracks and eating too much pizza?

"I was wondering if you could help me with something," you say, pulling out *Creepies*.

His eyes do a triple-take. He lowers his voice like you've just shown him a bag of pills instead of a fourth-rate *Ghoulies*. "Where'd you get that?" he says, and your heart sinks.

"I was hoping you sent it," you say to his already shaking head.

"No way. You know, that's our number one request but I'm not touching that thing. It's caught in a rights battle from hell."

"That never stopped you before," you say, noting several movies on the rack that will never again see the legal light of day due to said rights battles.

"They're not *Creepies*," he says, wincing at the word, like if he says it too many times, the puppets might show up. "This one's more complicated. Besides, it's . . . you know."

You shrug. No, you don't know.

He glances over his shoulder at Green Hair. "Cursed. That thing is cursed as shit."

You can't help but smirk. Maybe it's exhaustion. Maybe it's the fact that GFPP is a dead end. But smile you do.

"I'm serious," Matt says, "there's something going on with that movie."

"Humor me," you say, even if you're not in the mood for humor.

Green Hair brings over a stack of DVDs she'd like to purchase. Matt cuts her a deal, thanks her for the business, and sends her on her way. When she's out of ear shot, he sighs, like whatever he's about to say has been weighing on him. "It's a long story and I'm hoping to make some sales before I head out."

"Let's grab a drink," you say, "and I'll cover whatever business you lose. Besides, I see some movies I wouldn't mind coming home with. Maybe we do an episode on one. Maybe you get a shout-out. Who knows? Anything can happen."

That does the trick.

He grabs his coat and says he'll meet you out back in five. His girlfriend's up in the hotel room, drinking some whiskey to counteract the whiskey from last night. She should be down any minute.

Outside, it's as drizzly as ever. The sky is a dull white with gray thunderheads sprinkled throughout. There might be a storm in your future. You do as Matt says and make your way to the vendor and guest entrance. There's a bouncer on the steps, too busy playing his Switch and vaping to notice you. You brought your coffee along for the ride but you could go for something stronger. You toss it into the near overflowing trash bin. Something rummages from inside as if in thanks.

This part of town isn't the best. Case in point: the sirens in the distance and the man to your left using a carboard box as his sleeping bag. He mumbles something about a black void outside his windows. Must be some nightmare. Still, no one bothers you, asks for change or a cigarette, neither of which you have. You blow steam into your hands, kick your feet to get the feeling back. A couple third-rate actors and actresses make their way into the entrance. You recall years past, during the channel's infancy, when you walked through those same sorts of doors. Back then, you still wanted the fame, the attention. Now you feel more at home in your screening room with the black-out curtains doing their thing. Ray says you ought to join a dating site, get yourself back out there, but *out there* has never made sense to you. The real world seems to run on chaos. At least with movies, there's a pause button.

"Sorry about that," Matt says from the street corner, jogging your way. "Long night."

"Say no more," you say, and in your head you're thanking the stars he showed up when he did. You were just starting to think about Beth.

"There's a bar this way," Matt says, crossing the street. He glances at his phone. "It's early but I don't think it's the kind of place that closes."

You see what he means as you come upon a sports bar that likely hasn't renovated since it opened for business. Inside is a dimly lit skeletal space with just enough room for the bar, a dozen stools, and three grimy booths. The place is empty save for the gray-haired bartender and the gray-haired man at the farthest table, staring into his pint glass like there are answers to be found in the foam.

The bartender speaks with a gravelly voice. Her wrinkles seem bone deep, like if she managed a smile her face might just cave in.

She asks what you want. Matt orders a PBR and shot of Jameson. She turns to you next. You're what Ray would call a beer snob. You favor micro brewers from small towns no one's ever heard of. But this unnamed sports bar has precisely three taps. Two of them are Budweiser. The other is PBR.

"I'll have what he's having," you say, and soon the wrinkled woman sets down two overflowing glasses and just as many shots.

You propose a toast. "To *Creepies*."

Matt downs his Jameson but doesn't echo your sentiment. "I'm serious. That movie's fucked."

"Let's say I don't believe in curses," you say, feeling the whiskey's burn, wondering if what you said is true.

"I don't think it matters if you believe. You can *not* believe in lightning all you want. Doesn't mean you won't get struck. In this case, *Creepies* is the lightning."

"I got that part."

"You ever heard of the *Poltergeist* curse?" Matt says, nursing his beer, taking microscopic sips like he can delay what comes next.

"Sure," you say, "poor little girl died and so did a few others."

Matt nods. "Yeah, it's like that on crack. Everyone who appeared on camera in *Creepies* died within ten years of its release. You remember the stoner? He got impaled on a branch during a ski trip. Lost his balance on the way down even though skiing was his thing. And the jock? He crossed the street and got mowed down by a motorcycle. The guy driving said his brakes just cut out. He'd bought the bike three days before. Brand new. The final girl? She got launched out of a roller coaster at Six Flags. Her harness broke in half. The thing had just passed safety inspection with flying colors. I could go on."

You sip the PBR and belch up the taste of convention breakfast. The beer is mostly flat and room temperature but that won't stop you from ordering another. "What about the girl in the wall? The one that surfaces in the second half."

Matt shrugs. "No one seems to know about her. She's uncredited. In fact, she's the only character in the second half of the movie, unless you count that upside-down thing in the chair."

"So only half the movie is cursed," you say.

"Half a curse is still one too many," Matt says. He takes another mini-sip. It occurs to you he's probably not in a drinking mood on a Sunday morning after a weekend of partying. "Why're you so interested in *Creepies* anyway? You doing an episode or something?"

"Or something," you say, thinking of the notes you jotted down and also of Beth's soaked face as she surfaces from the water. You wish it were that simple, that she's just been hiding these last few years. You can practically smell the car's engine leaking onto the pavement, see the pine tree you collided with head on. You can feel the first sign of your cracked skull, sending waves of pain to every part of you and there's a ringing in your ears that will never stop. When you close your eyes to block that night out, you see Stoner and Jock and the others meeting their gory ends. Even though the puppets look silly by today's standards, there's something life-like about them, special effects with an emphasis on special. "I have to admit. That movie does get inside your head."

"I only watched it once," Matt says, "for the sake of curiosity. It's like a rite of passage, I guess. Me and a couple friends got stoned and torrented it. They thought it was stupid as shit. Not me. I couldn't stop watching. There's something about it, you know? Something that makes you *want* to watch. It might not be good in the normal sense but it's fascinating. I couldn't look away. Started feeling this pressure in the back of my throat, like someone was choking me or something. I tried to tell my friends but they were too baked to notice. When the movie faded to black, I saw someone in the television. In the reflection, I mean. There were three of us that night but I spotted a fourth standing behind the couch. It was fucking tall, like *freak show* tall, and its head seemed too big for its body. It was right behind me."

"Must have been some weed," you say.

"That's why I won't sell it."

"Thought you said it was the rights," you say through a crooked smile.

"Makes a great cover story," Matt says, eyes going in and out of focus. You wonder if he sees them too, the puppets with their blood-soaked mouths and claws.

"So it wasn't you who sent it," you say, deciding flat beer is better than no beer. You drain the glass in four square sips and the bartender's already pouring a sequel.

"Sorry to let you down," Matt says. He goes on to ask about the channel. You humor his questions because he's a fan and a subscriber and you owe him as much. But you're running on autopilot, giving one- and two-word answers. The rest of you is wondering about the remaining addresses and which of them is the right one, which of them sent you a movie you didn't realize would change you.

TEN

YOU TOSS THE OVER-STUFFED tote bag filled with GFPP "releases" into your backseat. You bought them at random, grabbing whatever you could for the hundred-dollar bill you set on the counter, right before you promised Matt a shout-out for the second time. There's a good chance you own most of them on VHS back in the studio but there's got to be one proverbial hidden gem in there somewhere.

As you depart from SpookyCon, you call Todd. He picks up on the second ring, like he's been expecting you, but the truth is you call him even less than Ray, which is approximately never.

"Everything okay?" Todd says. In the background, you hear screams. It's comforting to know he watches shot-on-video trash on his own time too, a reminder the channel is more than just a job.

"Everything's fine," you say, even if the jury's out. "I was just thinking, it might be cool to shoot a skit for *Creepies*, you know? Since it's our white whale. We could get in touch with whoever sent it, maybe have them in on the joke. And you're the one who opened it. Do you happen to remember a name or an address?"

Todd clicks his tongue, like he's rewinding the tape that is his brain. "Wasn't me."

"How do you mean?" you say, passing a Buick that's decided to drive thirty miles below the speed limit.

"I mean I didn't open it."

"You must have," you say, trying to keep the edge out of your voice.

"There was nothing *to* open," Todd says, pausing whatever kill scene he's in the midst of. "I figured it was you. I found the disc on your desk."

~

The rest of the drive is lost to you. The passing trees and gas stations and even your trusty old playlist are all just background noise. What you're thinking is obvious, that you must be losing your mind, which wouldn't exactly be the first time. But the problem with that theory is that Ray saw Beth on-screen too, even if he thinks it's a look-alike. So that part's real enough. Which leaves the matter of how the disc wound up on your desk, unnoticed for hours or days. *Creepies* is most collectors' holy grail, yourself included, meaning you would've noticed it sitting next to your coffee mug. At least that explains the stain. Something doesn't add up, but you're not sure what that something is.

Three hours later, you pull into the studio lot, kicking up snow and salt. You've been meaning to get it paved for years but rocks and mud have shot to the bottom of your priority list. The side stairs groan beneath your weight. Once inside, you call out for Ray and the others, just in case. The lot may be empty but on shooting days they catch rides or Ubers.

No one answers you. Which means it's not too late to cancel. Postponing the shoot will only cause more stress, more sleepless hours of frantic editing to release the video on time, but right now you're not concerned with getting the best take. You send a group text, letting the boys know you've come down with something. Your nose is leaking and you can't stop shivering. Ray asks if you need anything but you tell him you're fine. There's a can of chicken soup somewhere in the studio. You're not sure if they buy it, especially with your new-found *Creepies* obsession, but they don't exactly argue with a night off.

You search the kitchen because you weren't joking about that soup. Sure, you're not sick but you aren't well either. You find the can in the back of the cabinets, behind sugar and hot sauce. According to the date, it expired just under two years ago. You wonder what it would do to you, if it's any worse than a steady diet of pepperoni pizza and small-batch IPAs. You decide it can't be and nuke the can's jelly-like innards for thirty seconds. Then you put on a fresh pot of coffee.

The remaining addresses are still resting on the kitchen table. A half hour of internet sleuthing later, you come up with an email for each. You send a quick note, asking if they were the kind donators of *Creepies*. You make a joke of it to hide the desperation. The first one gets back to you in two minutes, says it wasn't them but they wish it was. They're such a big fan and keep up the good work. The second one arrives an hour later with more of the same.

You slurp your soup and coffee to the soundtrack of whatever's been scratching at the walls. It's closer now. It could be coming from the bathroom or the editing suite, but you know the sound will change position the moment you investigate. Let it scratch. You've softened these last twenty-four hours. You know what it's like to search for something that can't be found.

You yawn and rub your reddened eyes. The smart thing to do is nap for twelve hours but it feels like every moment sleeping is a moment wasted, like the answer you're chasing is drifting farther away.

Instead, you opt for internet archeology. What you're doing is searching for clues, like you're some private investigator instead of a mildly popular YouTube personality. What you find are dead ends. Matt Beaumont was telling the truth. Just about every actor from the first half of *Creepies* met their grisly end in both fiction and reality. But he didn't mention anything about the crew. You search for writers, producers—hell, even a grip would do. But much like Beth, they're all uncredited. Both directors are listed on IMDB as Alan Smithee, a notorious pseudonym used by anyone who's made a movie so embarrassing they'd prefer to keep it off their resume.

Does that mean *two* directors chose to remain anonymous? You want to call bullshit. This is the modern world. Nothing stays buried in the dawn of social media. You dig deeper, past IMDB and Wikipedia, past the popular horror news outlets, until you're sifting through amateur film blogs with white text on black backgrounds. The literary merit decreases as the typos increase. Pressure builds along the crown of your nose. Blinking hurts as much as breathing. You've never had a migraine, unless you count the night you fractured your skull, but you imagine it's a lot like this. Every horror fan who's seen *Creepies* likes to discuss the puppets and the kills but they seem to gloss over how this movie is as elusive as Nessie. And nobody seems *bothered* by this. They're happy to point out its flaws and baffling choices without pondering why the cast is dead and the crew have gone into hiding.

You close your browser and head for the worn-in couch. *Creepies* is still in the DVD player. The source material is all you have to work with. You pay close attention to landmarks but the opening sequence could've been shot in any overgrown country road this side of the Grand Canyon. There's a moss-laden street sign to the right of the frame. You pause and squint, tilt your head, but the words remain fractured. It could be Elm Street or it could be Washington Avenue. After that, it's the lawn in need of ride-on and the mansion in question. Just as our cast of unlikeables strolls toward the front door, something catches your eye in the background. You press pause once more. It's a water tower, ringed with small lights that make the structure vaguely UFO in nature. It could be any number of water towers but it bears a striking resemblance to one in your hometown, twenty miles north, in an area called Venus Hill, a popular spot for lovers and smokers. In high school, you and Ray would peer across the valley at the water tower, which always took on a green hue in the light of the stars. Much like those campfire nights, you'd concoct stories about the tower, how it wasn't really holding water but some strange substance recovered from the Mariana trench, a substance not original to Earth. It seems silly now but when you're baked in the heart of the night, nothing's out of the question. Just ask Matt Beaumont. But surely it's not the same tower. That would mean *Creepies* was shot not ten miles from your childhood home. And you, of all people, of all horror junkies, would've known as much.

Right?

ELEVEN

YOU SHOULD TELL YOUR PARENTS you're in town but you won't. It's been a month or three since you last visited. It's not that there's bad blood. They never hesitate to shower you with praise. In their eyes, you're as successful as Bill Gates. They're the ones who fostered your love of B movies. Most kids beg their folks for a trip to Disney Land. All you wanted was that four-for-three deal at your mom-and-pop rental store, the one they offered every Friday night as incentive. As if you *needed* incentive. And sure, everything close to popular was gone by the time you got there, but you weren't searching for popular. You wanted anything with a skull or a machine gun or both on the cover. Your parents would sit you down on the couch with a Coke in one hand and a microwavable bag of popcorn in the other. There, you'd watch whatever action, sci-fi, or horror tapes you opted for that weekend. Your mother allowed blood and guts but shielded your eyes at the slightest hint of nudity. With your dad, in true dad style, all bets were off. After each movie, they'd ask your thoughts on the model starships or rubber monster suits. They wanted you to understand *why* you liked this stuff. It's how you're able to speak with such authority, such depth, on films most people can't be troubled with. You owe your parents more than they know but a reunion isn't in the cards today.

You've got work to do.

It's been years since your last visit to Venus Hill, when you brought Beth up there like you were high school sweethearts. The hill's entrance is all but hidden, so subtle you'd miss it if it weren't branded in your memories. You take the exit slow, drive past a couple teens with backpacks that can only contain six-packs. Soon you're climbing an angle so steep, it feels like your car won't make it. The hill evens out to a grassless patch of land with a view of the valley ahead. There's the water tower. Even at this time of day, when the sky is riddled with ashen clouds, the structure still screams of alien design. If your geography is correct, you're a mile and a half west of the tower, which would put the mansion roughly the same distance to the east. You've never been out that way. It's a private road that branches off into other private roads. It's where the town doctors and lawyers and the mayor herself call home. And, it would seem, it's where both halves of *Creepies* were filmed. You wonder if the house is still decrepit or if someone's since gentrified the place. Maybe it was torn down after production wrapped. Maybe the curse died with it. Not that you believe in curses.

Through the passenger window, you spot the teens from earlier, winded from their walk. They pretend not to see you because up here, when you're underage, everyone's a cop. Soon, they vanish into the line of trees. You head downhill and turn toward the rich side of town.

The houses begin as ranches, then two-story colonials, and slowly transition to Victorians straight from a real estate bulletin board. The farther you drive, the farther back the homes become. Some are eclipsed by bare branches. You see suggestions of balconies and walk-out bedrooms, and you wonder what that's like. You make a decent living, don't get you wrong, but YouTube doesn't come with competitive benefits or a retirement package, and you're not the world's smartest saver. Beth used to needle you about this very issue. Instead of pre-ordering that new deluxe director's cut of a movie you own thrice over, why not open a high-yield savings? You always said you'd think about it, yet you never did.

Eventually, you pass the *private road* sign, and that's when things get barren. To reach any of the houses on this stretch, you'll need to traverse winding hills that most likely end in sealed gates with intercoms. You hope that's not the case with *Creepies* but either way, trespassing or no trespassing, you're seeing it in the flesh. You ponder at that last choice of word. *Flesh.* Some part of you has begun to suspect *Creepies* is more than just a movie. The other part, much like Ray, thinks you're off your rocker. The truth is likely somewhere in that murky in-between.

You pass a deadfall, where nothing has grown or thrived in decades, and spot in the distance a house as large as the others yet more fit for the Universal back lot. The windows have been boarded up and the paint's peeling like a bad case of eczema. Bingo. You pull off at the nearest road, which is more like a straight line of mud and weeds. One bumpy mile later you come to an overgrown field that could've once been a driveway. And on that field, only yards away, is the house where Stoner and company met their untimely fates. You kill the engine and look for signs of life. You doubt anyone watches over this place. It's probably kept in the family and whichever well-off relative has custody is content to let it rot.

Outside the car, you're slapped in the face with a bitter breeze. The temperature has plummeted. On your way to the front steps—most of which have grown bloated with moisture—you wonder what you expect to find inside. Even if *Creepies* was filmed here, and even if Beth once stepped foot inside, there are still far more questions than answers.

You don't think on it long, though, because your phone rings. Out here, the tone is loud enough to disturb a flock of crows from the nearest tree. They scatter through the overcast sky like buckshot and you wonder what brought them here. Aren't crows drawn to death?

You study your phone. It's Ray again. It's always Ray.

"Yeah?" you say.

"How're you holding up?"

For a moment, you wonder what he's talking about before recalling you're supposed to be sick. You fake a cough and a sniffle and doubt he buys it. "Good. I took a nap, did some editing. Business as usual."

Ray sighs. He knows bullshit when he hears it, but he won't say as much. Patience is his hubris. "You sure you don't need anything? I can pop over. I need to pick up some things anyway."

"No," you say too quickly. You don't want him finding the studio empty. You could always pretend you went home, to sleep in your own bed, but that's about as likely as finding left-over props in the house before you.

"Look, can I be honest with you?" Ray says next, and you know what's coming.

"I'm tired," you say, which isn't exactly a lie.

"I know what you're doing," Ray says, sounding suddenly like a lawyer, which makes you the defendant. "You're chasing ghosts. You've latched on to *Creepies* because of some blonde that looks like Beth's distant cousin. You're taking it as a sign because that's what you do. You make connections where there aren't any. You've come a long way and I don't want to see you fall back into old habits."

"I don't know what you're talking about," you say above the whooshing in your bad ear, because your pulse has taken to tripling its beat. It's disorienting, like your skull's full of water that'll never find its way out.

"But you do," Ray says. He sighs, groans, runs whatever comes next through his head. "She called me tonight. I wasn't going to say anything, but she called. She said you've been bothering her again."

"Who called?" you say.

"Beth."

TWELVE

"I'VE GOT TO GO," YOU say, ending the call before Ray has a chance to go on. For good measure, you turn your phone on airplane mode.

What you do next is step inside the house and wince at the way the front door creaks open. It sounds like a scream, like the remnants of a kill scene. It echoes above your tinnitus, then fades quickly, like something stifled it. Ahead is the front hall that leads to the living room on the left and the set of stairs on the right. If you're following *Creepies* in sequence, the living room's up first. What little sunlight breaks through the clouds keeps its distance from the house. You have to squint and even then everything's shrouded in inky blackness. Your eyes play tricks. For a moment, you see a grandfather clock, expect it to chime the hour, but another step forward proves the wall is empty. And above you, that chandelier is just some old water stain. You peer left. This is the approximate location of the pentagram, and while it looked etched into the wood on film, it's since been buffed out or painted over. Still, at the right angle, you swear you spot part of the outer circle and a point of the star within.

Inside the living room, you find the fireplace full of soot. It looks recent, like someone snuffed the flames only days ago. Not surprising. An empty house this large, you've got to assume the homeless have used it for shelter. You don't blame them. No one checks on this place. It's theirs for the taking. But you also wouldn't blame them for moving on quickly. The atmosphere is oppressive and then some. It weighs on you. Air seems scarce, like you've hiked atop a mountain without noticing. It's warmer than outside but it's not exactly the Ritz.

You flick on the flashlight app. The beam illuminates a miniature galaxy of dust particles. You're standing in the spot where the table and cooler would've been. You can practically smell the beer and snacks, hear the inappropriate synth music as the cast attempts to dance naturally. You pan your head slowly around the dusty room and when you pan back to the fireplace, your eyes glaze over with another jolt of static, like their tracking needs adjusting. It passes quickly. Probably some latent side effect of the plate in your skull.

You pause in the doorway. From here, the cast would've split up to investigate the house and the puppets hidden within, but it's this precise room where the second half of *Creepies* opens, and just above is where the infamous upside-down chair would've been. Your hair prickles. Part of you believes the chair is hovering above you. And that same part believes the figure's there too. When you risk a glance, you find a sagging ceiling, one with cracks and fissures but chairless just the same. You're about to let out a sigh you didn't know was building when a cloud of dust spills downward, followed by a sound that can only be footsteps.

You wipe bits of plaster from your eyes, back up into the hall, and find yourself at the foot of the stairs. You open your mouth to ask who's there but that would give away your location. It's better to stay quiet and get the fuck out of here. Before you have a chance, there are two shadows descending and you're sure now: this place is haunted. The cast may have died but they never really left. And logic follows that the puppets didn't either. Except when those shadows reach your level, you see not Jock or Stoner but the kids from earlier, the ones with backpacks. You were right about the beer. Each of them holds cracked-open cans, and each of them looks scared shitless.

"I'm not a cop," you say, just to clear the air.

"We didn't think so," the first kid says, trying on his best tough-guy accent. It needs work. It doesn't help that he hasn't grown into his ears, which jut out against the two-sizes-too-big baseball cap. His chin has sprouted precisely three strands of peach fuzz, strands he no doubt wears with pride.

"I'll take one if you don't mind," you say of the beer.

"We're all out," the second kid says. He's a foot taller and his voice is still in the process of changing. Every syllable comes out differently, alternating between low and high and cracking like arthritic joints. At some point, he must have broken his nose. It curves slightly to the left. He probably tells his friends it was a fight but it's more likely he tripped over his own feet. He doesn't seem like the fighting type.

"I'm not a cop," you say, "but I could *call* one."

They form a group huddle and decide forking over a beer is better than a ride to the station. Big Ears tosses one your way. It's a Rolling Rock. Cheap college stuff, even if the kids may be in junior high. You crack it open in their general direction, let the foam spray over them, then take a sip. It's warm and flat but it dulls some of your nerves, emphasis on *some*, because you're still inside the *Creepies* house. Speaking of which.

"You guys come here often?" you say.

They shrug, which is teenager for *I guess so*.

"You know there was a movie filmed here?" you say next, hoping the answer is *duh*.

"Yeah," Cracking Voice says, "a *shitty* movie."

"Hey now," you say, "shitty movies are kind of my thing."

"It's not *that* bad," Big Ears says. You knew you liked him. "At least what we saw of it. We shut it off when stuff started getting weird and because, you know, the curse and shit."

"Right," you say, "the curse and shit is why I'm here." What you don't say is the other part, the part about seeing Beth on-screen. Ray would have you believe it's just a coincidence. You should ask where his imagination went, that part of him that used to read ghost stories by firelight.

"There's no curse," Cracking Voice says, though he doesn't sound so sure. What gives it away is how his eyes dart right, then left, looking for the first sign of movement.

"Yeah there is," Big Ears says. "It's why all those people bit the big one." He must have heard the expression in a movie or television show, which tells you he's a lot like you. Sometimes it's easier to live life through fictional characters than to live it yourself.

"You mean the cast," you say.

He nods. "And the people who watch it."

"Hold up," you say, "what was that last part?" Another sip of warm beer and you feel it churning your stomach, like sulfuric acid, or maybe all the junk food has finally caught up to you. Maybe there's an ulcer in your future.

"That's just what I heard," Big Ears says, sipping from his own can, which has warped from his too-tight grip. "There's all sorts of stuff about it online, if you search long enough. Weird stuff happens to people who watch it."

"What kind of weird stuff?" you say, thinking you should hire him as a research assistant.

"Just weird," Big Ears says, and that's when Cracking Voice tosses his can onto the floor and tries to change the subject.

"It's just a movie," he says.

Big Ear's not taking the bait. "And this house is weird too. People say it just showed up one day. None of our parents remember it from growing up. I asked my mom about it one night and she looked at me like I was crazy. She didn't know what I was talking about. She never really does. I figured she just didn't want me coming here but then I tried to find it online. It's not even on Google. One time, we came out here to take pictures but they didn't work."

"What do you mean 'they didn't work'?" you say.

"Every time we looked at our phones, there was just static, like a glitch or something, like it doesn't *want* its picture taken."

"That's impossible," you say. "Look at this place. It's falling apart. It's been here forever." But tell that to your memory, to the who-knows-how-many nights you spent gazing at the water tower. You would've seen this place at least once.

Another teenage shrug. "I don't know what to tell you. All I know is the movie's fucked up and so is this place."

"No arguments there," you say, holding your stomach and praying for a belch to relieve the pressure.

"Why are you here anyway?" Cracking Voice says. "You a reporter?"

"Just a fan," you say, and wonder if it's true. Because while you waited three decades and then some to see *Creepies*, you're beginning to wish you hadn't. "You guys didn't see the ending? The girl who comes out of the wall?"

They shake their heads in unison and that's when you realize this is a dead end if you've ever seen one.

"Why don't you two get out of—" But before you reach *here*, there's more plaster dust raining down, more footsteps above.

You'd ask the kids if they brought friends but judging by the way they stampede out the front door, you're guessing that's a *no*.

You could go upstairs to prove there's no one there or you could follow their lead.

You follow their lead.

THIRTEEN

YOU DRIVE HOME, HOME BEING the studio, and put Google Street View to work. According to the date, the images were recorded five years prior. You type the approximate address of the *Creepies* house. At first, you see the field where the house *should* be, meaning it's not, but you probably got the number wrong. You type it again, and again, but all that shows up is a barren field sans mansion. You zoom until the image is as pixelated as Beth's face on pause, but there's still no house. You close the window and wonder what it means, how a house that size could've been built less than five years ago. And who designed it? Who decided to make it dilapidated from the start? Not to mention: how could it be a shooting location for a thirty-five-year-old movie? Unless someone took the time to move it by the foundation, and unless, by some miracle, it didn't crumble to dust in the process, there's no good answer.

Somewhere to your left, the scratching in the walls gets louder.

You busy yourself with checking the channel's email address. It's mostly fan mail with a healthy dose of hate mail. There's as much *You guys rock* as *You guys blow.* You delete most of it, not because you don't appreciate every supporter, but time is short and you're still a small operation. Among the generic messages are the rare personal ones, the ones telling you the channel got someone through a rough time, maybe even saved their lives. Those you respond to.

Two hundred emails later, as you're beginning to contemplate sleep, you find a message from Matt Beaumont.

The subject line reads: *Creepies info.*

You click. What you see is a series of links Matt has provided, all of them supposed articles or blog entries involving *Creepies,* but more specifically the strangeness that surrounds it.

Thought you'd find these useful, he writes. *Had a hard time sleeping since we talked. Have Creepies on the mind, I guess, which is the worst place to have them. I did some digging. I know you said you don't believe in curses but maybe this'll change your mind. And please don't watch that thing any more than you have to. Looking forward to the next episode—and the shout-out.*

You click on the first link. You're brought not to a horror movie blog but a site dedicated to "real life" paranormal accounts. Judging by the clip art and proprietary gifs, the site hasn't been updated since 1997, if ever. There's a quote at the top, something about the Illuminati and lizard people. After a few moments, the page loads a series of user entries. A scroll in either direction shows *only* user entries. It's a massive message board, like Reddit, only far less success-ful. The post in question is from an anonymous user who claims to have watched *Creepies* a whopping seventeen times, until their boot-leg, gray-market DVD stopped working and by "stopped working," they mean they placed the disc on the closest railroad tracks after what happened. Anonymous insists the film was not just playing with his head but manipulating reality itself. He began experiencing what he calls "intense and vivid flashbacks," all of which involved scenes from *Creepies*, but it was as if his mind believed they'd oc-curred in *his life*. He recalls being there in the living room with the cast, drinking their beer and smoking their joints, not just as a casual viewer but an active participant. The synchronicities don't end there. One day, he says, his living room took on a new configuration. He'd just stepped into the kitchen to make a sandwich and, upon return-ing, there was a fireplace in the far wall, beneath his flat screen TV. This was especially troubling since he didn't have a fireplace. When he next left the room and returned, he found the walls had been painted a dingy brown, as opposed to their normal sky blue. From there, the room expanded by several square feet. The ceiling rose. What Anonymous is getting at is his living room became the living room from the *Creepies* mansion. He goes on to say he knew the puppets would materialize next, but he didn't stick around to find out. He hired a moving company, paid extra for them to do the packing, and rented another apartment two towns over.

Crazy. Mentally unsound. Break with reality.

That's what you'd say if the last few days hadn't happened.

You read the comments and find several other anonymous posters describing similar experiences, how certain aspects of their lives began to mirror those of the characters within *Creepies*.

You close out of the site and choose another of Matt Beaumont's links at random. This one's from a Wells, Maine newspaper article. The reporter describes a "baffling and troubling" discovery in the local state park, where a mother and her three children found one of several playgrounds to be desecrated, which translates to spray-painted blasphemies, many of which deserve points for creativity.

God is watching and so is Satan.

The world will end not with a boom but a fart.

And your personal favorite: *Creepies is not a movie—life is.*

In addition to graffiti, police responding to the scene found dozens of stuffed animals, all of them gutted to reveal cotton innards. In the largest of the pack, a teddy bear whose eyes had likewise been gouged, police found an unmarked VHS tape peeking out. You don't need to read further to know what was on that tape.

From there, you learn you're far from the only one. *Creepies* has reportedly caused hallucinations, mass hysteria, several suicide attempts, and the list goes on. You make it through six of the links before deciding you've had enough ghost stories for tonight. You work on the newest episode for a while, forego things like food and water, until it's ready for a final watch-through. At the end of its roughly sixty-seven-minute runtime, everything looks good to go. You hit *upload* and step away from the computer.

In the screening room, *Creepies* is playing on mute, even though your TV should've shut off hours ago.

FOURTEEN

FINALLY, YOU SLEEP. YOU HAVE the lingering suspicion that nightmares plagued your dreams but each time you try to remember, there's only blackness. Much like the halfway mark of *Creepies*, you suspect there's something inside that void, something slowly taking shape.

Your phone is littered with unread texts from Ray. They're all of the concerned variety, though some take on an accusatory tone you could do without. The last thing you need is another lecture even if that lecture is warranted. You tell Ray everything's okay, then hop over to the group thread, where you inform the boys shooting will commence tomorrow. You're taking one additional mental health day, though there's nothing healthy about what you've got planned. Everyone says they're in if you're in. You tell them you might be scarce today. There's a lot of preparation before the shoot. The show is mostly improv but that doesn't mean you work from nothing. You can't be expected to remember all the facts surrounding the chosen movies. The same is doubly true for *Creepies*, since the facts might be fiction. There's also YouTube comments, more emails to answer, and a host of other responsibilities that go into having a successful channel. Most people think you just get drunk and watch movies. While that's still the heart of it, behind the scenes, it looks a lot like an office job, the same kind of job you fought so hard to avoid.

You eat a breakfast of coffee and nothing else and soon your phone's chiming again. It's Ray, of course, and this time his message is short but bitter: *please don't call her again.*

Instead of easing his worry, typing back *sure thing* or *you got it*, you shut off your phone. Your eyes once again glaze over with static. You wait for it to pass but it lasts longer than the other episodes. You should call a doctor but you've had enough doctors for a year, let alone a decade.

Three hours later, you've addressed just under one hundred comments, even some of the negative ones, though you always keep it cordial. It's good for engagement. A lot of channels can't be bothered with their fans but you owe them now and always. Without them, you'd still be months behind on your college loans, living off a maxed-out credit card you had no plans to pay off.

Next, you work through more emails. Three different indie directors have offered a free copy of their movie in exchange for an honest review. They've either never seen the channel or they have and only care about their art, using the term liberally. You could answer them instead of leaving them in limbo, but where's the fun in that?

Finally, you type some notes and a cheat sheet for tomorrow's shoot. You like to start with a skit, usually one that's intentionally awkward, but you opt for a cold opening this week. Recent events considered, you can't imagine cracking potty humor jokes or, you know, laughing.

You allow yourself a lunch break, lunch being a slice of hardened pizza you probably should've tossed a few days ago. It melts just fine in the microwave.

Without your phone, your playlist is inaccessible. It's too quiet for your taste, given the ringing and whooshing in your bad ear. You reach over to the boombox and that's when you remember you don't *own* a boombox. Yet there it is, resting between the coffee pot and toaster oven. It's an older model, one that screams 1987. These things are coming back, you know. A couple years ago, they cost five bucks at any garage sale. Now they're retro chic and sell for hundreds. What's old is new and all that. Out of curiosity, you press the *eject* button. Both tape decks are empty. You check the cord to find it unplugged, but that doesn't stop you from pressing *play*. What comes out of the tinny speakers is somehow exactly what you expected. It's not your playlist and it's not talk radio. It's the inappropriate synth music from the *Creepies* dance scene. The track plays for a minute or two, never switching up the tempo or structure. It almost fades to background noise until the synths are replaced with harsh drones, the ominous cue that signals the film's second half. You press *stop* and like any good horror movie, it doesn't. You press it again as a formality and then you knock it to the floor, let your shoes do the talking. Six or seven stomps later, the stereo's seen better days. The plastic's chipped and the wiring within peeks through the new cracks. But the music hasn't gotten the memo. In fact, the music's *louder*, doesn't seem to be coming from the boombox but from all around you. It masks your tinnitus but the scratching manages to break through the cacophony. You lift the boombox by the cord and toss it off the balcony, toward the sets. It crashes, breaks apart in a blast of plastic shrapnel, but the soundtrack doesn't skip a beat.

The drones drone on.

When you turn around, there's a fresh boombox on the counter.

FIFTEEN

YOU TRY WEARING HEADPHONES BUT the drone finds a way through. No amount of soundtracks or podcasts do the trick. Next you resort to ear plugs. They dull the sound some but it's still there, still in the background like white noise that won't quit.

"You'll have to try harder," you tell the boombox, and perhaps the scratching too. What you mean is you've been through this before, for years at a time. You know what it's like when the *off* button has malfunctioned. You know what it's like to have a constant reminder of one poor decision, one bad night to end all others, and you've been fighting back ever since, putting all your angst and woe-is-me into the channel. So if *Creepies* wants to test you, let it. And speaking of *Creepies*, you open Matt Beaumont's email once more and sift through the rest of the links.

In the early nineties, via a shady back-alley transaction, three high school students in Indiana scored themselves a VHS copy of *Creepies*. They attempted to film their very own fan-made sequel. Since they couldn't afford actors, they cast themselves, and since they couldn't afford latex, the puppets were fashioned from paper bags and oven mitts. When they watched the project back on their television sets, instead of what they'd filmed, they saw *themselves* lying face down in their parents' dens and finished basements, heads crushed, wounds soaking the wall-to-wall carpeting. Nearby sat the amateur puppets with googly eyes that seemed to peer toward the camera.

A video store in Philly managed to track down a copy of *Creepies* from a collector's personal liquidation sale. They charged three times their usual rental fee, knowing the value and allure of the film. A young man named Steve was the first to rent the tape and, it would seem, the last. One night, after closing, Steve returned to the shop with a can of gasoline. He broke through the display window, doused himself, and lit a cigarette. Firefighters were quick to respond, but by the time they stopped the flames, the man was barely more than a skeleton. Officials on the scene stated "it looked as though he'd burned steady all night" as opposed to the twelve minutes it took first responders to control the blaze. Most of the shop was destroyed save for the back room, where the copy of *Creepies* sat unharmed in the unsorted returns bin.

Finally you come to the last link, yet another newspaper article. This one's about a car crash not far from the studio. It describes a man in his late twenties and a woman—the man's girlfriend—of approximately the same age. The couple had gotten into an argument that night. There was a 35mm screening of *Friday the 13th Part 3D* at the Hawthorne Theater in Marlowe, Massachusetts. The man had always wanted to see the slasher on a proper silver screen, where the 3D effects would look as they were meant to. The woman wanted a quiet night out at her favorite Thai restaurant. She was "movied out." Can you believe that? Who could possibly tire of movies? The man promised he'd make it up to her. She agreed with a roll of her eyes. The film was even better than the man had hoped for. The audience cheered at each and every cheap three-dimensional gag. The man ate popcorn and drank vanilla Coke until his gut grew distended. To each of those Cokes, he added a nip or three of middle-shelf whiskey, which he'd smuggled into the theater by way of his backpack. By the fifth or sixth, he was starting to feel it. What he should've done is let his girlfriend drive, like she insisted, but he got carsick in the passenger seat. He drove slow and took the back roads. He was just three miles from the woman's apartment when the brakes locked.

Don't they say the worst things happen closest to home?

You didn't see that tree, the one on Dead Man's Bend, which got its name from all the people who took the sharp turn too fast, just like you did that night. Upon impact, you hit your head hard enough to shatter the driver's-side safety glass. You noticed an immediate ringing in your left ear. When you peered to your right, Beth wasn't talking, mostly on account of the way her jaw had become dislocated. The way the blood flowed, it seemed never to stop. You remember thinking it wasn't possible to have that much blood in one person and also how fragile we all are, like living, breathing water balloons. All it takes is one strong push or shove and everything meant to stay inside comes cascading out. You figured she'd die that night, and maybe she did in a sense, because three reconstructive surgeries later, she didn't look like Beth anymore. She told you in the simplest terms she'd never forgive you, no matter how many apologies or grand gestures. And that's all you've wanted since that night: forgiveness. You're not asking her to take you back. But each time you reach out, despite the eventual restraining order, she doesn't hesitate to remind you that forgiveness isn't in your future—or hers.

Static filling your vision again, your mind tuning to a station that's gone off the air. And the droning of course. And don't forget the scratching.

You blink and find yourself not at your computer but on your trusty couch, watching a group of teens search for the perfect spot to party.

SIXTEEN

IT'S TUESDAY AND YOU KNOW what that means.

You and Ray and the rest of the gang will order takeout, split a six-pack (or drink one each), and sit in front of the television in the screening room. There are two films to discuss but the Rambo knock-off is just an appetizer.

There's only one movie that matters tonight.

Or any night.

Someone knocks at the door. You figure it's the boys but instead it's the pizza delivery guy, the one you vaguely recognize after all these years, yet whose name you've never bothered to learn. In fact, until now, you've never given him a proper once-over. You search his chest for a name tag but come up empty. Outside, clouds bruise the sky and the sun is scarce but the man bears a striking resemblance to Stoner. You wink at him, like you're in on the same joke, and you can't tell in the dimness if he looks confused or winks back in secret acknowledgment. You tell him to keep the change.

The boys should be here any moment. The polite thing to do is wait but you've worked up quite the appetite watching *Creepies* for the sixth or seventh time. There was no reason for another viewing, not when you'll be watching it again tonight, but you don't *need* a reason. You open the top-most pizza box and note with disdain that they've botched your order. Instead of pepperoni, they've slathered the pie with olives. You try the next box to find ham and pineapple. The final one's not much better unless you like mushrooms, which you definitely don't. But your stomach's not in the mood to be picky, and upon the first bite of said mushrooms, you're not quite revolted. It doesn't taste half bad actually. Kind of earthy. Some part of you wonders if that's a good or a bad sign, if suddenly favoring your least favorite food is another indication of something odd happening. But your vision cuts out in what's now familiar static, and when you regain consciousness, you forget what you were thinking about. All you know is the pizza is finger-licking tasty.

Another knock at the door as the boys let themselves in, carrying enough beer to stock a liquor store. They approach you like you're an improvised explosive device, like you might go off at the slightest wrong move. You smile and tell them it's about time.

"You feeling okay?" Ray says, the bravest of the bomb squad.

"Never better," you say around a mouthful of your favorite piz-za. The sauce drips from the corner of your grinning mouth, not unlike blood.

The boys eye the open boxes, furrow their brows like something's wrong, but they keep quiet.

"Before you ask," you tell them, "the boombox is broken. That's why the droning won't stop. And as for that scratching, I'm open to theories. I thought it was a mouse but it sounds bigger now. Maybe he's been eating my crumbs."

Ray strains, as if listening for something in the distance. "What droning?" he says.

From behind, Todd does the same. "And what scratching?"

"Don't worry about it," you say, "let's get to work."

~

You crack open two beers since one seems like a tease. Ray hovers in the doorway while the others prepare in the screening room. You shake your head, tell him not to bother. You're in no mood for consoling. You're tired and winters are hard, especially in New England, where the darkness is plentiful. It feels like the world is shrinking, so that only this place exists, so that you could never leave. Not that you'd want to.

"We could cancel," Ray says. "Film another night. It's no big deal."

"What did I just say?"

Ray tenses and even though you feel bad, even though he's basically your brother, you can't help it. You've grown tired of being under his microscope, a specimen to study while more and more variables are introduced to your tank. Tonight you're shutting down the experiment.

"Everything's fine," you tell him. "I went home last night. Slept like a puppy." The lie comes more freely than the truth and maybe it's been that way for some time.

You can't be sure if he buys it. He cracks a quarter-hearted joke you instantly forget and grabs a beer. You follow him into the screening room.

Halfway through the action film, you've already killed a bag of pretzels, half a tube of Pringles, and four slices of mushroom pizza. Your stomach gurgles. It's not enough. It needs more. You wonder if this is what it's like waking from a coma. Your body keeps working while the rest of you takes a vacation. And when you come back, your body's a stranger. It doesn't trust you at first. Breathing seems foreign and your joints are stiff no matter how much you stretch. As a peace offering, you eat one more slice and a handful of Cheetos.

You're each cracking jokes and discussing certain sections of the film because the cameras are rolling now. This will be the seventy-sixth episode. You're a seasoned pro, already editing the video in your head. You know which parts you'll cut and where you'll insert clips of the film. Between this segment and the round-table discussion that follows, you've got eight to ten hours of work ahead of you. People don't realize how much time goes in to just one episode. To the casual viewer, it's like the events happened in order but to you, it's long hours of grunting in frustration and resting your eyes because they refuse to focus.

Static blurs your vision as if in agreement.

The action film ends and everything's going great. The boys have brought their A game. You can already tell this one's a success. You break for more snacks and more beer. In the kitchen Todd's waxing poetic about the old days, how his grandmother's basement smelled of menthol cigarettes, about the time you discovered his grandfather's porn collection from the sixties. A small misshapen box in the closet you all deemed the Bush Basket. You smirk and pretend what comes next is like any other film you've ever watched.

Back in the screening room, Todd presses play and you're met with the opening of *Creepies*, the cast of unlikeables making their way to the haunted mansion. You mouth the words of Stoner and Jock and Sluts One and Two. No one else seems to notice. They're rolling with laughter and it's genuine this second time around, not played up for the public. But you know what comes next. The fun will be short-lived. You wonder if they'll see it too, the liquid wall where Beth has been all this time.

It's coming. The second half of *Creepies* is coming. Stoner's about to meet his end on the sacrificial slab.

"What the hell?" Todd says.

He's pointing toward the screen, where the film has given way to blackness.

"Is the disc scratched?" Eric says.

You shake your head *no*.

Your mouth whispers on its own accord. It's saying things you don't quite understand in a language you've never heard before. The scratching is louder even if none of the boys seem to notice.

Todd presses *play* again to no avail.

Eric shakes the DVD player like that'll do the trick.

It's Ray's idea to eject the disc, inspect it for dust and scratches. There's nothing he can see as he angles it toward the light but all it takes is one impurity.

Your mouth mumbles that *Creepies can't* be broken, that it was created in such a way to never stop playing. After one viewing it's *in* you, floating through your bloodstream and metastasizing. Just ask the cast, if there's anyone left. Or the crew, whoever they may be.

Ray slides the disc back in and presses *play* for the final time. The second segment begins. There's the POV and the pentagram. The empty living room and its small crackling fire. The stairs and hallway and finally the wall with its oceanic movement. Wood paneling for only a moment before the transition to liquid. You can't move your head or your limbs or even your eyes as the shot zooms on the face about to emerge. The boys have taken their seats, have all stopped moving and speaking and perhaps breathing. You wonder if their noses are bleeding as well. You taste pennies dripping down the back of your throat because you're not just in the screening room anymore. You're in two places at once. The other is the front seat of your mangled car, holding the side of your swollen head as it leaks onto the leather interior. Beth's mumbling something with her broken mouth. In the distance are the police cruisers and the ambulance and the jaws of life that will pry you from the vehicle you just paid off.

The shot draws closer.

The ripples expand.

The boys notice. You sense their awe. She's beautiful. Beth is beautiful. She's lifting herself out of the silver pool and calling to you. You've all but forgotten her voice, since she refuses to answer your calls, but you kept an old voicemail of hers, something benign about going shopping. Each time you listen, you're shocked how different she sounds. Lower or higher than you'd once thought. Sometimes, when the ringing gets too bad, when a fan or white noise machine won't do the trick, you play the message on a loop.

But you don't need that voice anymore. You've got the droning and the scratching—static blanketing everything with gray and black specks—and you've got *Creepies*. Your fingers tingle as the feeling comes back, as the film allows you to move once more. From your pocket, you retrieve your phone and delete the voicemail. Then, sifting through your contacts, scrolling past hundreds of unanswered text messages, you delete Beth herself. If she won't forgive you, perhaps the Beth on-screen will.

A new notification pops up. It's from Matt Beaumont.

I watched it again. Creepies, *I mean, but you knew what I meant. I found a copy sitting on my coffee table, asked my girlfriend if she knew where it came from but she was too hungover to hear. I didn't want to watch but every time I tossed the thing, it showed up again. In my cabinets and between my couch cushions and even beneath my pillow, like I'd been a good little boy and the tooth fairy had favored me. I'm there now. In the mansion. The chair's floating just above me and so is whatever's sitting in it. I can almost make out a face, a mouth that's far too long. I don't have the time to count its teeth but trust me when I say there's plenty. I can hear the puppets too. Even though this is the second half of* Creepies, *I know they're still around here somewhere. They've just gone into hiding. Something tells me it's almost time for them to re-emerge. Something also tells me they won't look the same. I think what we saw in the first half, that was just a disguise, their masks. And we all wear masks, don't we? We only show the ones we love our true faces. I tried to show my girlfriend mine but she didn't understand. At least she won't be hungover anymore. You feel it, don't you? You feel the screen opening like a door and that door doesn't open for just anyone. So make your choice. You've been selected. You've been offered a gift. Take it from someone on the other side, it's the greatest gift of all. I've got to go now. The thing above me is whispering. You wouldn't believe what it's saying, what it knows, what it's capable of. You'll find out—*

Crying.

You hear someone crying.

It's Ray and Todd and Eric, all of them paralyzed as you were, all of them sobbing like children at their grandmother or grandfather's funeral, their first taste of true dread and sorrow. You'd tell them it's going to be okay but that's a promise you can't keep.

What you *can* do is stand from the couch and drop your phone since you won't be needing it. You can rest a hand on each of their shoulders and tell them it's been a wonderful ride. The channel has meant everything. It's so hard these days to make your own way, to find steady cash from anything other than a soul-slurping conglomerate that cares more about profits than your emotional well-being. Most people trudge through their lives without ever feeling a sense of accomplishment. You should each be proud of what you've done here, in this studio, in this screening room. You've watched hundreds of films that would've been forgotten otherwise. In many ways, you're a team of historians, cataloguing media that has slipped through the cracks of popular culture. With any luck, future generations will take up the torch.

But not you.

There's only one film left to catalogue.

"We found it," you say. "We found *Creepies*."

Or, more precisely, *Creepies* found you.

SEVENTEEN

BETH EMERGES FROM THE WALL of water. She steps toward the screen, toward *you*. This version of her isn't scarred or deformed. Her jaw is set perfectly and she can smile just fine. You wipe your nose with the back of your hand as more blood trickles down your throat. Beth shivers. It must be cold wherever she's been. And dark. Darker than your brain cells could ever interpret. But there's room for two and she's been waiting a long time.

So have you.

You head for the kitchen. The boombox is droning on but suddenly it's not loud enough. You crank the volume and nod your approval. Above it all, above even your ringing ear: the scratching, what you thought was an intruder but now know to be an invitation.

As you pass the screening room, you hear the moans of your

channelmates. You're not sure if the sounds signal ecstasy or agony or perhaps a healthy dose of each. On-screen, Beth's gone now, her wall of water static—*static* like lightning across your vision. You follow the general direction of the scratching. It's closer than you thought. It's coming from the editing suite, the room where you spend most of your time because make-believe makes more sense than reality. Watching yourself on-screen is easier than staring into a mirror. That other version, that Internet doppelganger, is who you *wish* you were when the cameras turn off. You grasp the knob and find it cool to the touch, like the studio's heat has malfunctioned, but the cold is coming from somewhere else, and when you pull the door open, you see where.

Gone is your desk, the one you cursed over for twelve hours, wondering how a civil engineer could understand the instructions let alone a professional YouTuber. Gone too is the computer, with its three screens and ergonomic keyboard. The room has been swapped for a wall made entirely from television snow, the same snow (*static*) you've been seeing for some time now, since your first viewing of *Creepies*, though it's hard to imagine a time before *Creepies*. It feels like that part of your life, the *before*, was all just practice, leading to the *after*, to the *now*.

You know what to do next. Follow the sound of the scratching because the scratching is *them*, calling out, inviting you in.

You reach a hand forward, toward the snow, *through* the snow. It's like submerging your fingers into jelly, like being reborn. The digits tingle again. Not from paralysis but from your cells changing, reconfiguring for what comes next. You recall all the movies you've watched on this side of the static, how they kept your anxiety and depression at bay, how they more than likely saved your life. How fitting, then, that your life should become one. But enough self-reflection. It's time now. Time to push through the sticky substance of the screen, until you're elbow deep, shoulder deep, then shoving your head into your new home.

And your new home is the front hallway of the *Creepies* house. You're standing beside the pentagram. Behind you, the doorway now leads to nothing. The static has been turned off and whoever did the turning off doesn't want you leaving. In its place is pure blackness, the absence of all light and stars, like everything outside the mansion has burned away for good. If you leapt into the void, you'd never stop falling, never hit the bottom of wherever it might lead. Better to stay inside then. It's not like you've got anywhere to be. The pentagram glows an odd shade of green, like a light source has been placed behind it. It warms you some, waves you on. Don't mind if you do.

You step down the hall, boards creaking and groaning with each footfall, and find yourself in the living room.

It isn't empty anymore.

There's a party going on and you're invited.

The stereo from the kitchen has made the trek with you. It rests on the table between all the essentials: booze and snacks and more booze.

Jock nods your way, muscles bulging the fabric of his two-sizes-too-small high school football jacket. Whatever the team's name is, it begins with a C. "What took you so long, dude?"

"Sorry," you say. Your words are lost when he presses *play* on the boombox. The off-kilter synths return but the droning remains. It's like the tracks coexist, like they were meant to be played in tandem. And maybe *Creepies* is like that too. Maybe the two halves add up to something bigger.

Sluts One and Two ask if you're thirsty. You're about to say *no* but they're already handing you a fresh beer. The words on the label read as gibberish, like plopping open a book in the bowels of a dream. The bottle wasn't in either of their hands a blink ago but that doesn't matter. What matters is the beer's cold and crisp and goes down easier than anything you've tossed back recently. You belch and they laugh.

Stoner's up next. From his breast pocket he pulls out the fattest joint you've ever seen. "You up for it?"

You shrug.

He smirks. "I knew I liked you, man. Some people are so closed off. They don't believe in anything they can't see and touch but reality's a slippery-ass sundae and what we see is only the cherry on top. We've got to grab that spoon and dig deeper. It's all about expanding your mind, right?"

"Sure," you say as he sparks up and lets you do the honors. The smoke doesn't burn your lungs like all the other times you've gotten baked. You hold it in, let the calmness wash over you, then blow it back in his face.

"Far out," he says before launching into another cosmic diatribe.

A tap on your shoulder. It's Punk, with his stereotypical mohawk and lip ring, connected to his eyebrow ring by way of a silver chain. Much like the label on the beer, you can't read his shirt, but you get the gist from the burning American flag. Down with authority.

"You heard us," he says in awe, like he thought you'd never show.

"You should've knocked louder," you say, pointing to the left side of your head. "I've got a bad ear, you know."

"Hell yeah." He salutes you with finger devil horns. That's the universal sign for metal, not punk, but the directors, whoever they may be, wrote him that way. He's beholden to his creator.

Finally, there's Final Girl. She stands alone in the corner because, like any proper FG, parties have never been her thing. The beer she's holding is just for show. What she's thinking is she'd rather be home studying. She doesn't realize she *is* home.

From deep within the house's heart: a shuffling sound, a noise that's more like a harbinger. The music screeches to a record-scratching halt. The cast eyes each other, asks if anyone else heard that, when the sound makes its return. Of course you heard it.

"Let's check it out," Stoner says. "We'll split up to cover more ground."

"That's a terrible idea," Final Girl says from her corner, her words unheard.

You can't help but smirk.

"You in?" Stoner says, already heading for the basement and the slab he doesn't know will end his screen time.

"Right behind you," you say as the group filters out.

Final Girl lingers the longest. "I have a bad feeling about this," she says, her horror movie sixth sense working overtime for no pay.

"It'll be fine," you say. Technically, it's not a lie. Technically, you'll never know.

She sighs, mutters "Fucking great," then the thirsty shadows lap her up.

EIGHTEEN

YOU HANG BACK IN THE living room, wait for the fire to be lit, wait for the second half of *Creepies* to announce its arrival. In the distance, the screams begin as the cast is picked off one by one, except Sluts One and Two, who meet their end at approximately the same time by way of a chainsaw found on the kitchen table of all places. The puppets can barely lift the saw, let alone grasp the handle, but movie logic is a beautiful thing. From here, you can't *see* the puppets, with their knock-off *Gremlins* scales and *Ghoulies* fangs, but you've committed them to memory. Besides, if Matt Beaumont was right, what they look like now is about to change.

You toss back the rest of your beer, which maintains its carbonation and perfect sipping temperature. You eat chips with the precise amount of salt and crunch and pace around the room, killing time, assuming time exists here. You peer through the closest window to study the darkness again. Is it moving, rippling like the surface of Beth's wall, or is that just how your eyes interpret it? Are you alone in the vastness of this place or are there other mansions with other puppets?

From behind, the fireplace sparks to life as the final scream echoes through the halls. That would be Stoner and his slab and the geyser of blood that follows. When you turn, the fire's going steady and the snacks are gone. The droning reaches fever pitch, loud enough to make you wince, but it won't hurt you. If anything, it masks the ringing. In this place, you'll never have to worry about tinnitus again.

Upstairs: the sound of splashing.

That's your cue.

You pan across the living room, your eyes the camera now, and continue into the hallway. The pentagram's glowing has dimmed but it isn't any less menacing. You take your time. This is a long continuous shot after all. You marvel at the set's detail, how each wall's water stains and peeling paint set the mood. Some would call it eerie or unnerving but you're no snob. You prefer the term "spooky as hell."

You reach the stairs and hold the shot, let the audience begin to lose their patience, ready to fast forward. You begin to ascend, each step threatening to splinter beneath you. How many times has the cast made this climb? How many more to come?

At the top, you follow the hallway, linger in each doorway, building tension. It's almost time but this isn't about the payoff. It's like Hitchcock said: there's no suspense in an explosion, only the ticking of the bomb. And that's what makes *Creepies* so special. We may never know if the timer reached zero.

One bedroom down.

Onto the second.

Pause.

Take it all in.

And now the third, as you step inside and slowly zoom on the far wall, where Beth is, where she's always been. Any moment, she'll emerge. You have so much to say to her. Or perhaps this Beth already knows. Perhaps she's aware that you, too, lost something in the crash, that you, too, never forgave yourself. Your eyes flood with tears. More blood tickles your throat. The hairs along your arms and neck stand tall.

The air charges, as if a storm has entered the atmosphere, and in a sense it has.

It's a storm you've been chasing for years.

And it's here.

It's—

Not moving.

The wall isn't moving like it's supposed to. You step farther into the room, reach out a trembling hand, but touch only bloated wood that vibrates beneath your palm. You knock but nothing knocks back.

"No," you say, "you're supposed to be here."

You push, hoping for a secret lever or button, but the wall remains a wall.

"You promised," you say.

"Don't bother, man," someone says from the corner, mostly blanketed in shadows until they step forward, at which point you lose that crisp beer and those perfect chips all over the warped floor.

It's Matt Beaumont—or it was at some point. What's left of him isn't holding up so well. For one, he's developed a terrible hunch, his neck and head pointing at an angle that can't be comfortable. Secondly, his arms have grown elongated, nearly reaching his ankles, which are bloated and bruised. And that brings you to his face, using the term relatively. His left eye is three times larger than the right. The pupil has engulfed the iris and the white, so that it doesn't look so different from the void outside. Every inch of his pale skin is bulbous with varicose veins, moving beneath the surface like eels.

"Crazy, right?" Matt says, his voice octaves lower than the last time you spoke. His lips are swollen and raw and you can only imagine the teeth within have also undergone a transformation.

"What happened?" you say, backing away to your own corner, the one where Beth is supposed to save you.

Matt shrugs—or at least you think he does. It's hard to tell with the hunch, with the way his top half is too heavy for his too-thin legs, which now bend the wrong way. "Hell if I know. Last thing I remember is whispering, more words and syllables than all the languages combined. He knows the answer to every secret and all you have to do is ask. Now I'm no expert—" He snickers at this and ooze the color of infection drips down his jutting chin. "But I think he has special plans for me. I think what's happening is I'm becoming one of *them*. One of the Creepies."

"Who's 'he'?"

More laughter. It sounds cruel now, like the rest of the class has seen the note taped to your back, but whatever's scribbled on there is still a secret to you. "Mr. C. Who else?"

"The second director?" you say, wondering how many steps it would take to spring for the door, wondering where you'd go from there.

"Director. God. Call him the mayor if you want. It's all the same. He's so glad you're finally here." Another chuckle as Matt holds his stomach with a talon-like hand, the fingers fused together. "You didn't really think it was Beth, did you? You didn't think some angelic version of your long-lost love called you here." The larger of his eyes widens before amphibian lids blink shut. "You *did*. You poor son of a bitch. I thought you came here because you wanted to. You really fell for it."

"No," you say, shaking your head. It's a lie. A prank. Beth called you here. You saw her on the screen and so did the boys. You don't deserve this. You deserve forgiveness.

"Good luck with that," Matt says, from inside your skull and out. "You should be honored. From what I hear, you aced the audition. What the film was missing was a movie nerd. You know, the stand-in for the audience. The one who loves horror movies, knows them inside and out. The one who spells out all the terror and madness before it happens. You got the part, man. Now, we're dealing with a microbudget, so we can't offer you much in the way of money, but the food's not half bad, and it's all about the experience, right?"

"Why?" is all you can manage around your sobbing throat.

Matt wipes slime from his mouth but there's plenty more to take its place. "Why don't you ask him yourself?"

From above, warm and foul air washes over you, like the breath of some beast that can never be sated. You nearly forgot the upside-down chair and the upside-down figure. He's there. The second director is there. Mr. C is there. You don't have enough adjectives or metaphors in your vocabulary to describe his features, to make sense of his geometry, but you do know he has a mouth larger than any you've ever seen, and that mouth is headed for you.

NINETEEN

THE CHARACTERS ARRIVE AT THE mansion and kill the engine. Jock's been driving, complaining about how bored he is. He steps out and finishes off his road soda, crushes it against his forehead and tosses it into the weeds. We cut to a POV shot of something low to the ground. Something roughly the size of a puppet creature. It doesn't like the litter on its home turf and shows as much with a deep grunt. Cut back to the kids and Jock's straining to hear.

"What was that?" he says.

"What was what?" Punk says. He rolls his eyes. "Let's get moving, okay? Place gives me the creeps."

"Thought I heard something," Jock says.

Stoner pats him on the back. "And you said I was the paranoid one. Come on, let's do this." He's carrying a boombox in one hand and a Ziploc overflowing with weed in the other, though it looks more like oregano and catnip.

Hard cut to Nerd, a man in his mid-thirties, wearing a torn and faded horror movie shirt that hangs off his thin frame like sagging skin. He's deathly thin despite his constant diet of junk food. His friends like to tease him, ask him where he finds the room in his stomach for all that garbage. It'll catch up to him, they say. The left side of his head is slightly misshapen with a hairless scar, as if he was once injured in an accident. Something about his ear seems to be bothering him. He looks exhausted. He looks frightened. He looks lost.

"You know," Nerd says, "they say this place is haunted."

Nobody listens.

They never do.

Acknowledgments

Special thanks go to the finest of fine folks at Grindhouse Press, my fellow authors slapping their keyboards like they might scurry away elsewise, and all the labels unearthing films of video stores past to grant them physical releases. Also, without my parents allowing me to watch horror, science fiction, and action films at a much-too-young age, this book ends up not existing. Thank you, Mom and Dad, for always looking the other way during movie night. And Emily and Nora? Who's lucky enough to have a wife and daughter that not only tolerate a larger-than-average physical media collection but embrace it? Me, apparently, but it's more like I'm lucky to have *them*. Lastly, the elephant in the YouTube studio is Red Letter Media, a channel that's not only provided me with near-infinite hours of entertainment but changed the way I think and talk about movies. They're that rare species of film critic that lack even trace amounts of pretentiousness, who champion all things schlock and A-for-effort, all filtered through a healthy cynical lens. There's no BMN without RLM.

Patrick Lacey was born and raised in a haunted house. He spends his time writing about things that make the general public shiver. He lives in a hopefully un-haunted house in Massachusetts with two hyperactive cats, his daughter, and his wife. Follow him on Twitter (@patlacey).

Other Grindhouse Press Titles

29278639R00073